Flurry the Bear

The Rising Tide

J.S. Skye

The Rising Tide
(Flurry the Bear – Book 5)
Copyright © 2015 J.S. Skye
All rights reserved.
www.FlurryTheBear.com

Cover art by Luís Figueiredo, J.S. Skye, & Tony Washington

ISBN: 0692478051
ISBN-13: 978-0692478059

CONTENTS

CHAPTER 1
CLASH OF WILLS

BOOM! One cannon cracked after another. The atmosphere was filled with smoke and ash. Pitch-covered splinters flew in every direction, driven by the explosive force. High-speed projectiles of debris were flung about from each impact of the cast-iron balls. Ocean waves chopped to and fro, slamming oak planks against the hulls of the feuding ships.

Shouts and screams blanketed the continuous clanging of metal on metal. It was a fight to the death! The two pirate ships battled to the bitter end, and the outcome was now down to the duel of the captains.

Captain Fineas was nearly the victor, but he had one last task. He had to end the threat of his evil nemesis, Captain Crabtree. Fineas's crew stood by as their commander took up arms without any intervention. Fineas's shipmates were loyal to him, and they held true to their time-honored tradition of allowing the captain to finish the fight against his foe alone.

With a swing of their swords and delivered punches, the battle was fueled by their ever-increasing rage. The skirmish was so suspenseful that Flurry clutched the arm of the couch with a death grip. Even though it was just a movie, the little bear cub felt like he was really there. It seemed as if he could smell the smoke, taste the salt water, and feel the heat from the burning sails.

Flurry cheered his scale-covered hero onward. As the white teddy bear watched the television set, he could not take the suspense any longer. Flurry desperately waited for the moment of truth while the captains stared each other down with their spiteful gazes. Flurry leaned in closer to the screen. Caboose scooted closer to Flurry and grabbed his arm.

The pirate captains were near the end of their duel. They raised their swords for one final advance. Captain Fineas ducked beneath his enemy's high-handed swing, drew his sword back, and ... *CLICK*

"Mommy! I was watching that!" Flurry shouted indignantly at his mother, who stood behind the couch with the television remote in hand.

"Flurry, where did you get this movie? I don't remember buying this. What ever happened to your Captain Ju Ju Bear movie? I thought you loved that one."

"Awww, Mommy! That movie is so boring! This one is so much better, and it was just getting to the good part!" Flurry's disappointed tone saturated the room.

Caboose shrank away, quietly slipped off of the couch, and dashed out of the room. Noah observed from the dining room table where he had been drawing. Noah watched and shook his head. He knew that would happen. He tried to warn Flurry, but did Flurry ever listen? No!

"This movie is rated PG-13. You're not thirteen years old, mister!" replied the cub's mother.

"But the Ju Ju Bear movie is for kids! I don't like it anymore. This movie is so much better!" Flurry replied in a whiny tone. He sounded like a moping child rather than someone old enough to watch such a violent movie.

"Flurry, you're still a kid! I know you think you're older, but you're not!"

"I'm not a child anymore!" he shouted.

"Then why are you acting like one?"

"Why are you acting like one?" Flurry repeated mockingly in an altered voice.

"Don't you start with me, or you're going to find yourself in serious trouble!" Flurry's mother had a scowl on her face and her arms crossed. "You never answered my question. Where did you get this movie?" She was quickly losing her patience.

"I got it for free," replied the cub with an annoyed sigh.

"Got it for free? Where? How?" After a brief pause, she continued. "Out with it!"

"I downloaded it off of the Internet," Flurry mumbled.

"Wait a minute! You pirated this movie?" Her face was beet-red with anger.

Flurry thought she kind of looked like Captain Crabtree now, if not due to her red face, then for the fact that she certainly felt like his adversary. *Good thing she doesn't have crab-like pincers, too*, Flurry thought to himself.

She looked at the cub and could tell he had retreated into his own little world inside his head. "Hello? I'm speaking to you!"

Flurry snapped out of his thought and replied, "No, I got it for free." Flurry's response seemed innocent enough, though frustration could still be detected in his tone.

"No, Flurry, it's not for free! People worked hard to make this movie. Do you know how much money goes into making a movie like this?" After a brief moment of silence, she quickly resumed. "Well, do you?"

"No," came his whisper of an answer as he looked down at the floor.

"Flurry, the people that make these movies have families of their own. They have to pay bills and put food on the table. It costs a lot of money to hire people to paint the sets, sew costumes, and build props. The actors probably spend twelve to sixteen hours a day between acting and getting makeup put on or taken off. Then there's the cost of lights, cameras, and other equipment.

Someone has to compose the music. There are people that edit the footage. Marketing a product costs a lot of money as well. When it's all said and done, many movies cost millions of dollars to make, and instead of paying them for their movie, you just took it. That's piracy! You stole from them!"

"But pirates are cool, Mommy!" Flurry was not sure what was so wrong with being a pirate. In the movies, the pirates always looked so cool to him.

"No, they aren't. Pirates steal what doesn't belong to them. Would you like it if I stole all of your chocolate?"

"No, I guess not," replied the downcast cub.

"Flurry, I just don't know what to do with you anymore. Ever since your first trip back to your hometown, you haven't been the same. What has gotten into you?"

Flurry teared up. He tried to wipe the drops from his eyes, but the water freely flowed as he ran off to his bedroom.

Flurry's mother looked up and saw the other fuzzies staring back at her. Boaz and Honja had both come out from wherever they had been hiding to join their brothers, and it was clear that nobody knew what to say. Flurry's mother sighed and made her way to the cub's room.

Flurry lay under his bedspread and sobbed. He heard a rapping at the door, followed by his mother's voice. "Honey, it's late. You've had a long day. Maybe you should get some rest, and we'll talk about this in the morning along with your father."

Flurry did not reply; he simply continued to mope and sniffle from under the covers.

His mother stood at the threshold and rubbed her eyes. The stress of being a mother wore on her at times such as this. Flurry's brothers entered the room and prepared for bed.

With a softened expression on her face, their mother entered the room, tucked all of them in, and gave them each a kiss on the cheek, followed up with a hug. She finished with Flurry. She pulled his blanket down from his head, wiped away his tears, and laid his head on the pillow. Lynn looked upon her furry boy with compassion. She stroked his head, pulled the blanket back up to his chin, and kissed him goodnight before she walked to the door. "Goodnight everyone! Sweet dreams. I love all of you very much!" After their individual replies, she flipped off the light switch and closed the door behind her.

Flurry lay in his bed in the darkened room, lit only by the nightlight on the opposite wall from the window. Flurry pondered their argument. He was uncertain why she was so upset. Flurry thought pirates were the greatest things ever, and he did not see why his new favorite movie was the topic of contention. After all, the movie was mild compared to what Flurry had been through already. For only being a teddy bear cub, he had seen more than most people have seen in an entire lifetime.

By now Flurry was incredibly fatigued, but his mind raced with so many thoughts of possible voyages. His thirst for adventure was insatiable. It was like an unquenchable fire, and with each passing day, it consumed him more and more.

It had been three months since his last adventure at the side of the red panda samurai known as Tomodachi. The previous adventure had rekindled something in Flurry that had yet to subside.

Granted, his experiences were frightening and downright traumatic at times, yet he still craved it. It was an addiction. Flurry even felt like he could justify future adventures, now that he had been speaking with a counselor about his frequent nightmares.

Flurry's parents managed to make an arrangement for him to get therapy over the phone, since it would not be possible to take a living, breathing teddy bear to the therapist's office. The world was not ready to discover there are some teddy bears that are actually alive.

Flurry lay in bed and thought about his

cherished pirate movie, but his eyelids became increasingly heavy. While he dozed off, he mumbled the words, "I wish I could go on an adventure of my own." Before he knew it, he was fast asleep.

Morning came, and Flurry was roused from a good night's sleep. His eyes were still closed, but he could tell that his mother must have left the window open, because he could feel the wind blow against his fur.

However, it was strange to him that his mother had not come in to make him get out of bed. He thought he would take advantage of the situation and snuggled back up under his blanket. While he remained in a cozy bundle, he heard the birds chirp and the sound of water flow. *Wait a minute!* Flurry thought to himself. *Why am I hearing the sound of water in my room?* In an instant,

Flurry's eyes were wide open. He turned his head and beheld that he was still in his bed, but it floated on an open body of water.

Fear took hold of him. "What in the world?" Flurry shouted. He sat straight up and yanked the blanket away. His sudden movement made the bed bob up and down among the shallow waves. Flurry was so confused. *How could something like this even happen?* he puzzled.

Flurry looked all around in the hope of getting his bearings. The only familiar sight was that of his plush brothers, fast asleep in their own beds. They, too, happened to be floating alongside him.

"Guys! Guys! Get up!" Flurry bellowed. They awoke, and were just as startled as Flurry was.

"Uh, Flurry, what's going on?" Boaz

asked while he rubbed his eyes. He put his glasses on. His brain tried to make sense of their circumstances, but it kept coming up short.

Honja was dismayed. When he saw the water, he responded with an immediate dive back under his blanket. If you did not know Honja was beneath his bedspread, you would have thought shook with fear on its own.

Noah sat in silence with his paw to his chin. He pondered their unique circumstance. Caboose was so enamored by the water that he was not paying attention to the others. He stared at his own reflection and made different faces at the fellow that stared back at him from below. Strangely enough, the other furry face always made the same expressions as Caboose. *Sat polar bear always knows what I'm going to do next*, Caboose reasoned in his head.

After a long pause, Flurry realized that Boaz had asked him a question. "Oh, sorry. What did you say? Oh yeah! I don't know how we got here." Flurry felt the need to defend himself so he added, "I didn't do it!"

"Let me guess, Caboose did it?" Boaz sarcastically remarked, since Flurry was notorious for blaming everything on Caboose.

Before Flurry could answer, Caboose enthusiastically answered for himself. "Uh huh, I did it!"

"What? That isn't even possible!" Flurry shouted. He was quite dumbfounded that Caboose would say such a thing. Then Flurry felt a bit of remorse when he recollected that he was primarily responsible for Caboose's conditioned response. After all, Flurry had blamed that cream-colored plush for a great many things over the past year. It would seem Caboose had heard it so frequently that he now believed it himself.

"Caboose, you didn't do this!" Boaz exclaimed.

"Oh..." Caboose replied, a little confused. He then added, "Are you sure?"

"See what you've done?" Boaz addressed Flurry with an angry glance. The little lion had buried his face in his paws out of sheer disbelief that Caboose thought himself responsible for their mysterious relocation.

Boaz was deeply concerned about their situation and decided to speak up again. "We need to figure out what to do. I don't like the idea of being lost at sea." The others nodded in agreement and looked to Flurry for a response.

Noah waved to Flurry and pointed out toward the opposite horizon. Flurry, Boaz, and Caboose all turned and looked. What they found came as such a relief. Their gaze fell upon land ... and a lot of it. They were not as far out at sea as they initially believed. In fact, the land was merely a stone's throw away. The coast had an extensive beach, backed by a forest and a port city of some kind. There were boats and ships that came and went all around them, but they had been so focused on each other that they did not notice they were not alone.

In fact, a ship closed in on them while they sat and deliberated about what to do. Flurry and Boaz shot a look of concern at each other. They knew very well they were in the ship's path.

"Quick! Paddle toward the shore! We have to get out of the way!" Flurry shouted. The bear got on his belly and paddled, but he could not progress at a fast enough pace.

"Guys, this would go much faster if you helped me!" Flurry chimed back in with frustration in his voice. He knew his little arms would not get him very far without some help.

Boaz then realized that Flurry's bed was the farthest away from the ship's path. The wooden beast barreled down on them. The small lion did not want to alarm the others, but he had to convince them to abandon their beds.

"Come here, Honja! We need to all get on Flurry's bed. You'll be safe with us there." Boaz tried to instill confidence in his timid friend. Honja peeked out from his blanket.

When he saw the water, he drew back inside his makeshift sanctuary. "Honja, please! You don't want to stay out here all alone, do you?"

Honja looked out at the waves and shook his head. Little did Honja know what hastily approached him from behind. Boaz jumped over to Honja's bed and picked him up. "I know you don't like this, but I have to do it. It's for your own good," Boaz reassured the tiny brown bunny rabbit.

With Honja now safely in his arms, the short lion plush leapt from bed to bed, until he reached Flurry's. Noah and Caboose had already arrived while Boaz had been trying to coerce Honja's compliance.

"Great! Now that we're all here, let's paddle to shore," Flurry commanded. He glanced up and saw the ship was nearly upon them. "Quickly!" he added in a hysterical voice. Normally the others would not like to follow his orders, but at that particular moment, Flurry's plan was as good as any.

The four plush cubs paddled hard while Honja hid in the middle of the bed. It looked like the ship would plow over them. The massive vessel cut through the waves, and submerged four of the little beds. It narrowly missed Flurry and his friends by only a few feet.

The brothers sighed with relief at the near miss. Flurry was pleased to see that the waves from the ship had helped to push them out of the way and toward land. With the momentum from the ship's wake and the help of the others, they quickly approached the shoreline.

The gang was overjoyed when Flurry's bed ran ashore. Honja leapt to the safety of solid ground at the first opportune moment. Noah, Boaz, and Caboose disembarked as well. Flurry quickly became enamored with the beautiful city that stood before them with the dense forest all around. The tree leaves were hues of orange, yellow, and red. Autumn was in full swing, and the cool breeze from the wind swept loose leaves past their feet.

Boaz investigated. Upon analysis of the architectural design, Boaz deduced that the city was oriental in origin. After he looked the place over, he turned his attention to Flurry. His gaze fixated upon the cub with the blue scarf. "Well?" Boaz asked.

"Well, what?" Flurry replied.

"What's next?"

"Why are you asking me?"

"You always want to be the leader, don't you? So lead!" replied the plush lion.

"I guess we go into the city," Flurry answered. He had a hint of insecurity in his voice. To Boaz, it sounded like a question rather than a statement. Flurry looked to Noah for support, but the tall, slender fellow simply shrugged.

Flurry always liked the idea of being the leader and giving all of the orders, but making decisions that could possibly be wrong haunted him. His pride made him anxious about mistakes or looking foolish in front of others. The only thing that could have made him any more uneasy would have been the presence of Drizzle. Flurry was glad he was at least spared the humiliation of looking dumb in front of that particular cub.

It was odd that Flurry put so much stock in what Drizzle presumed about him. Only six months prior they were on opposite sides of an unstable and volatile partnership. Flurry had never liked him. To Flurry, Drizzle was strange and the most unique bear he had ever met, and that made Flurry uncomfortable.

With an uneasy grin, Flurry finalized his decision. "Okay, let's go. Maybe we can at least find out where we are."

Flurry and the others headed toward the oriental city not far ahead of them. As they approached, they noticed that most of the inhabitants were tigers. Many of the large felines were well-dressed in their fancy decorative robes, and they walked upright like men.

There were many other kinds of animals present. Even some humans could be seen out and about, which Flurry did not see often. Flurry remembered from school that the animal races were typically known to stay far away from humans, and humans did likewise.

A young woman watched them intently as they entered the streets. In fact, Flurry thought she observed their every move, but he tried to pretend that he did not notice. Flurry was quite the actor, and he put on another show to pretend that he knew where he was going while he led his gang of plush animals forward.

From time-to-time, Flurry would glance back at the young lady. Flurry felt there was something peculiar about her. She seemed familiar somehow. He observed her slender frame and features closely. She had long, straight hair. Each strand was dark brown. Her eyes were also brown, with stripes painted across her face at eye level.

The woman reminded Flurry of the Native American people. His mother had read about them in one of his adventure books. Their female observer was very beautiful. She wore a strange necklace fit snugly against her throat. It appeared to be made from bamboo, but Flurry was not sure. *That can't be comfortable. How can she even breathe?* he thought to himself.

Before long, Flurry's attention was redirected when they found themselves in a marketplace. He briefly looked back, but the lady was no longer there. Flurry shook his head and focused on the vendors, who had stalls filled with novelties of every kind.

Absolutely anything could be found among the merchants if you looked hard enough. Flurry's eyes widened when he gazed upon the piles of fruit, weapons, clothing, pastries, jewelry, and many other items of interest.

The smell of freshly baked goods triggered Flurry to lick his lips with desire. He approached one of the vendors, but Noah tugged on his scarf.

"What?" Flurry asked.

Noah waved his arms and made a motion with his paw that indicated neither he nor Flurry had any money.

"Right, good point, Noah," replied the bear. "Maybe nobody will notice if we just take one."

"No!" Boaz interjected. "That's stealing! Mommy would be very angry if she knew you were even suggesting such a thing."

"But I'm hungry! She wouldn't want us to starve," Flurry reasoned.

Boaz was not swayed. He stood with his arms folded and replied, "Flurry, we're all stuffed animals. None of us need to eat anything. You can't justify stealing to live, because it's impossible for you to starve!"

Flurry giggled uneasily and then muttered quietly, "Speak for yourself." He felt embarrassed that Boaz had exposed his flawed logic. With a sigh, Flurry relented. "Fine! Let's go."

Before Flurry and the others could even turn their backs on the stall, the vendor yelled, "Hey! You have to pay for that!"

Flurry spun around and found Caboose gnawing away at a pastry. "Caboose! Oh no!" In the heat of the moment, Flurry bellowed, "Run!"

The fuzzies darted off as fast as they could. The angry merchant chased them through the streets and shouted, "Thief! Thief! Catch him!"

Under the legs of bystanders and over various obstacles, they ran. Before long, the vendor gave up when he realized he could not keep up with them. After the angry baker turned and walked away, Flurry and the others took refuge behind a crate and panted for breath.

"Caboose! Why did you do that?" shouted Boaz and Flurry in unison. Noah shook his head in disbelief.

Caboose simply replied with his lisp, "Sat was yummy!"

All four of his brothers had buried their faces in their paws. None of them could believe what Caboose had just done, or that he did not seem to understand that he was now a thief.

"Great! Now we're criminals," Boaz announced to the others.

"No, just Caboose. We didn't do anything," Flurry replied.

"That's where you're wrong. We all ran, so that makes us his accomplices."

"What's an acco … accomy?" Flurry uneasily asked.

"An accomplice is somebody that helps someone else commit a crime," Boaz replied with intense frustration in his tone.

"Yeah, I knew that!"

Boaz made an annoyed groan and clenched his paws. Dealing with Flurry often took a tremendous amount of patience, and Boaz's was wearing thin. "Well, the good thing is that we …" Boaz stopped short and looked to and fro. "Wait a minute! Where's Caboose?"

"Again?" Flurry hollered for his friend, "Caboose! Where are you? Caboose!"

"Caboose!" Boaz joined in.

Flurry's posture relaxed. "There he is!" He sighed with relief and pointed at some crates a few yards away. Caboose stood there petrified by a butterfly that had landed on his nose. His eyes crossed, while he stared down his snout at it.

"Caboose!" Flurry and Boaz called out together while they ran toward him.

"Don't wander off like that!" Flurry lectured the polar bear, as if Flurry had any room to tell others what not to do.

Caboose had now become too enthralled with his little winged visitor to pay any attention to his friend with the blue scarf.

Noah suddenly looked concerned. He pointed to something. The others looked and saw a guard patrolling the area. "Oh no! What if he arrests us?" Flurry asked his friends, but when he turned around, he discovered that they were absent.

"Pssst! Flurry! Over here! Hurry!" hissed Boaz from behind a crate. Flurry dashed for cover. They waited some time behind the crates until they thought the coast was clear. "Okay, I think it's safe now," Boaz told the others, but once again, Caboose was gone. "Oh no! Not again!"

Boaz was about to call out for Caboose when he spotted him at the side of the dock.

"This is going badly! Somebody needs to keep a closer eye on him," Boaz informed the group. Honja replied in his own language, and Noah nodded his head in agreement. The three brothers looked intently at Flurry.

Flurry realized that they expected him to watch after the polar bear. He sighed, got up, and walked toward Caboose. As he made his way between the crates, Flurry bumped into a bystander, who shouted, "Hey! Watch where you're going!"

Flurry froze in his tracks. "Wait a minute! I know that voice." Flurry then murmured to himself, "Please, don't be Drizzle. Please, don't be Drizzle." He turned around and looked up to find none other than Drizzle. "Of course! Just my luck! It just had to be you, didn't it?" Flurry shouted in frustration. "Could this day get any worse? Why, yes! Now Drizzle's here! What next?"

Everyone looked uncertain what to say or do. Drizzle decided to step in and inquire,

"Flurry? What are you doing here? On second thought, what do you mean by any of that?"

The others came out from behind the various shipping crates that littered the dock. Drizzle still looked as adorable as ever with his black fur and red scarf. However, he now carried a sword at his side.

Flurry sighed. He did not know how to answer him, so he looked to Boaz for some help.

"We don't know how we got here. In fact, we don't know where 'here' even is," said Boaz.

"Well, this is the city of Tigris," Drizzle replied.

"What are you doing here?" Flurry asked.

"I'm here with my friend."

"Friend? That's a good one! What friend?

Since when do you have friends?" Flurry insensitively commented.

Drizzle's feelings were clearly hurt, but before he could answer, someone behind Flurry cleared his throat loudly enough to gain the bear's attention. Flurry spun around and saw a young red panda. The figure stood before him with a sword strapped to his back and a decorative gauntlet on his right paw.

"Chingu!" Flurry shouted, and then turned back to Drizzle and said, "Why didn't you just say it was Chingu?"

"What other friend do you think I would've been referring to?"

"Yeah, good point," Flurry replied.

"Excuse me, I don't mean to interrupt, but there are a lot of unanswered questions," Boaz interjected. "I mean, we don't know how we got here, where our home is, or how to even get back. Any help would be appreciated."

Chingu opened his mouth and prepared to speak, but Drizzle spoke up first. "Chingu and I are on a mission to find his brother. He disappeared only moments ago. Then …"

Drizzle was cut short when Flurry looked back at Chingu and said, "By the way, how's Faith?"

"Hey! I was talking!" shouted Drizzle.

Chingu's eyes narrowed. He reached for his sword. Flurry was clearly perplexed by the red panda's actions. The cub felt prompted to take a step back. Five pirates approached their position from behind. The leader, a hyena, walked up and asked, "Well, well, well, what have we here?" Flurry and the others turned and saw the rest of the pirates: a panther, a brown bear, and two black wolves. All of them looked dangerous. Their paws rested on their swords, ready to draw at a moment's notice.

"What did you do with Shinyuu?" Drizzle shouted at their visitors.

After a chuckle, the hyena replied, "The red panda I knocked out while he was fighting three of my shipmates? Ha, ha, ha, ha, ha! That fool is on our ship over there." He nodded in the direction of a sea vessel and continued. "It's the same ship we're taking you to."

"No, you're not," Chingu chimed in.

The hyena abruptly stowed the smile from his face, stood up straight, and glared right at the red panda. "Who's going to stop us? You?" The others laughed. He pulled out his sword and pointed it at Chingu's nose.

Without any hesitation, Chingu did a

quick backflip and yanked his sword from its scabbard. The bandits laughed and all drew their swords as well. Flurry and his friends took cover behind the crates while Drizzle and Chingu stood together.

"Drizzle! Drizzle! Get out of the way!" Flurry shouted from behind the shipping container.

"I'm not abandoning my friend," Drizzle replied.

"Go! I've got this," Chingu assured Drizzle.

Drizzle stepped away, and Chingu separated his sword into two blades. He stood ready, with a weapon in each paw. The brown bear looked concerned and told the others, "That's the legendary sword of Tomodachi the Great. This one must be the Protector!"

"I don't care who he is. He'll look great stuffed and hanging on the bulkhead of our ship," the hyena replied.

The hyena lunged at Chingu. As quickly as he made his move, the pirate dropped to the ground, lifeless. The others attacked, and Chingu cut down the panther and the bear just as swiftly. Fear filled the hearts of the two wolves that remained. They turned and made a run for it. Chingu put his blades back together, stowed his sword, and pursued them.

Through the marketplace they darted. The pirate duo toppled crates, shelving, barrels, food stands, and anything else they could find to obstruct the red panda's path. The wolves ran so hard they could barely breathe. Down the city streets, through alleys, and around corners they dashed.

When they looked behind them, they found no trace of their pursuer. "I think we lost him," one of the wolves said as they took a turn down a dark alley.

With his back up against the wall, the second wolf peeked around the corner. "You might be right, I don't see him either."

They both let out a sigh of relief, turned around, and saw Chingu standing behind them. He pulled his sword and dispatched the thugs promptly as they futilely tried to defend themselves.

Back at the dock, Flurry and the others were still in danger. When Chingu had chased after the black wolves, a few other shady characters had showed up. Flurry knew they were part of the same gang of pirates. The cubs all tried to run, but the shipmates caught Flurry and his friends.

"You're coming with us," growled one of the thugs. Flurry and the others relentlessly tried to call out for help while they were stuffed into a burlap sack. The pirates loaded their captives onto a rowboat and headed for one of three large ships a short distance from the docks.

The boat was on its way before anyone could process what had just happened. Off it went toward its destination. A ship waited for its new cargo. Chingu arrived a moment too late. He stood on the dock and watched helplessly as his friends were ferried away.

CHAPTER 2
SOUND STRATEGY

The longboat cast off toward its mother ship before any of the cubs could process what had happened. Out further from the port sat three foreboding ships that lay in wait, as if they were predators stalking their prey. The pirate captors pulled their oars hard against the jostling waves. Flurry and his friends were tied with ropes, and sat on the floor of the boat. A menacing shadow engulfed all of the passengers. Flurry looked up and saw the massive vessel that towered over them.

Flurry, Drizzle, Noah, and Boaz watched as their captivity drew closer to being permanent. Caboose was unaware he should be concerned about anything. He was content to play with the puddle of water he sat in. Honja shook and cowered behind Boaz.

Their captors dragged Flurry and his gang out of the small boat and up to the deck of the ship. Normally, Flurry would have been overjoyed to board a pirate ship, but he was not in the best of moods. "Take them below and lock them up!" came the command of a fellow shipmate from the diverse crew of ruffians. Multiple pirates approached Flurry and his friends, removed their ropes, and used the tips of their swords to prod the cubs toward a set of steps. Flurry and Drizzle traded concerned glances while they were led along and brought below deck.

They descended into the belly of the wooden beast. Flurry noticed the crew was quite varied. Most of them were rodents or other types of scavenger animals. Flurry was keen on the fact that there were also some heavy hitters, like the panther who stood on the deck and glared at him before Flurry was forced to go below.

A rat stood at the helm. The captain's hat, which sat upon his furry head, made his position of rank perfectly clear. He shouted out orders to his crew. The sailors dashed about the ship and made all manner of preparations to set sail. In no time at all, the rat captain gave his final command. "Weigh anchor!"

The ship's menagerie replied, "Aye!" Members of the crew worked together and turned a large wheel which raised the anchor from the depths. The crew made ready to depart, but as the anchor broke the surface of the waves, it dragged up something else along with it.

Clinging tightly to the chain hung a red panda. Help was on the way! Chingu snapped his head back forcefully to release the excess sea water from his fur. He gazed up at the ship, narrowed his eyes, and with a hint of a grin, he softly spoke to himself, "Now it begins!"

Below deck, Flurry did not know what to think. He felt perplexed by everything that had happened since he awoke. In fact, this day had been the most bizarre day of his entire life. *Surely, this is just a dream*, he surmised. "Wake up, Flurry! Wake up!" he muttered and slapped himself in the face.

"Hmmm … That didn't work. Maybe I need to hit harder."

Flurry was about to slap himself again when he heard, "Here, let me help you with that!" Drizzle's statement was quickly followed up with a smack across the back of Flurry's head.

"Ouch! Drizzle! That isn't funny!" The other fuzzy members of the group showed that they disagreed with his statement when they all giggled. Flurry's face was surely red under his shiny fur.

"Oooh! A game!" Caboose turned toward Flurry and smacked him on the leg.

"Caboose! This isn't the 'Slap Flurry' game!" Flurry's frustration was clear, though the others all chuckled anyway.

The merriment would have continued if not for the guards. "Keep quiet or we'll silence ya ourselves!" They each looked up and saw one of the pirates make a cutting motion with his knife. Flurry and his friends got the message loud and clear. Honja's legs trembled, and tears formed in his eyes. The rabbit buried his head in Boaz's chest for comfort.

The trip into the bowels of the ship took longer than Flurry expected it to. They traveled down deep to reach the hold, and then to the aft section of the deck that housed the brig.

"Get in there!" shouted one of their captors. He shoved Flurry and his friends into a small cage and locked it shut. The guard left the room and closed the creaking door behind him. Drizzle had excellent hearing, and he easily made out the muffled voice of the pirate telling the other guard,

"Keep an eye on 'em! If any escape, it'll be your head!"

"Aye, sir!" came the guard's reply.

Drizzle sighed and plopped down to the wet deck. "What now?" Drizzle's broken spirit was all too apparent.

"How am I supposed to know? You're the genius!" Flurry sarcastically replied.

"Would you two stop bickering for just one second?" Boaz snapped. "Seriously though, what are we going to do?"

Noah joined the conversation. He pretended to shoot a rifle he now held in his paws. He then acted out a sword fight and followed it all up with a boxing act.

"Noah, I'm not in the mood to play these games," Flurry answered. The bear dropped to the wooden floor next to Drizzle and pouted.

"Uh … guys, where did Noah get that rifle or the sword?" Boaz asked. He was so perplexed. It seemed as if Noah made them appear out of thin air, and then they were gone as quickly as they came to be.

"What are you talking about?" Flurry asked.

"Am I the only one who saw that?" Boaz replied. Caboose looked around, clearly confused by the conversation. Honja hid under the polar bear, still frightened beyond words.

"Are you the only one who saw what?" Drizzle asked.

With a sigh, Boaz answered, "He isn't playing a game, he thinks we should fight our way out."

"Fight?" Drizzle exclaimed with a tone of sheer surprise. Noah gave him the thumbs up and nodded his head in agreement. "How are we going to do that? In case you couldn't tell, we're locked up, and we don't have any weapons."

"You sure about that?" Boaz made his snarky comment. "It looked like he had weapons just a moment ago, but apparently nobody else saw it." Boaz continued with much sarcasm and frustration in his tone. "Nearly nine months of this, and nobody ever sees it," the lion cub muttered to himself.

Noah pointed at Honja and the space between the cage bars. Honja shook his head. The rabbit then covered his head, and cowered down under Caboose again.

The brig had many prisoners strewn about. For the most part, the others were chained up and shackled to the bulkhead or

J.S. SKYE

to the deck. Only a few others, besides Flurry and his gang, were in a cage. A majority of the captives were polar bears, with the exception of one red panda balled up in the corner of the cage. None of the fuzzies had given much attention to their fellow inmates.

Drizzle scanned the room. He nearly passed over the fellow who slouched in the shadows. A look of recognition blanketed Drizzle's face. "Shinyuu? Is that you?" he asked.

The red panda turned, looked up, and replied, "Oh, hey, Drizzle!"

"Wait a minute! You two know each other?" Flurry was shocked beyond belief. He could not understand how Drizzle kept making new friends. In Ursus, Drizzle was often ignored and disliked for being

52

different, but now he knew the unlikeliest of characters.

"Yes. Why do you seem so surprised?" Drizzle responded. Flurry did not know what to say. He simply shrugged in reply to Drizzle's query.

Drizzle turned his attention back to his friend. "What happened to you? I thought you were winning that fight, and then you vanished."

"I thought so, too. Then there was that punch that blind-sided me. Next thing I know, I was out cold. Now I'm a captive, like everyone else down here."

"When do you not get captured?" asked a voice from the shadows of the brig. A figure stepped forward into the light and revealed itself to be a sopping wet red panda.

"Chingu!" shouted Flurry, Drizzle, and

Shinyuu in unison.

Chingu instantly threw up his paws and motioned for them to be still. "Quiet down, or I'm a comin' in there!" came the bellow of a guard from outside the door.

In a whispered tone, Flurry and Drizzle continued. "What are you doing here?"

"How did you get on the ship?" Flurry inquired.

"How did you get past the guards?" asked Drizzle.

"Why is he so wet?" Caboose added. Shinyuu chuckled to himself in amusement at Caboose's question.

Chingu shook his head and sighed. He pulled out a rolled-up piece of leather from his side pouch. He unrolled it to reveal an array of metal instruments. The red panda chose two of them and picked the lock on the cage. Before long, the gate creaked opened. Everyone in Flurry's gang were free.

"Who says we need a key?" Chingu commented.

Flurry and the others all ran out and gave him a group hug. "Okay, okay, that's enough," whispered Chingu. As soon as they let go, Chingu rushed over and unlocked Shinyuu's shackles.

Shinyuu jumped up and hugged Chingu tightly. "You're my hero," Shinyuu said in a sarcastic tone. When he let go, Chingu smacked him across the back of the head. "Ouch! Why do you always do that?"

"I'll stop doing it when you quit getting captured," Chingu answered.

"Fair enough," Shinyuu replied and rubbed his head.

Flurry stood there, watched their interaction, and wondered what was going on. "Would someone please explain?"

"Everyone, this is Shinyuu. He's one of Chingu's brothers," Drizzle introduced.

"Brothers?" Flurry asked. "I didn't know you had brothers."

"I have six, in fact," Chingu replied.

"Six?" Flurry loudly exclaimed, followed by everyone hushing him to be quiet. "Oops!" Flurry whispered. He thought about how one sister was more than enough for him. He could not even begin to imagine having six.

Chingu nodded and walked over to the polar bear prisoners. "Where are you from?" he asked.

One of the downtrodden polar bears spoke up. "We're from the southeastern tip of Urs. It's far north of here, where it's colder. We were on a mission when our ship was attacked and burned to ash by Black Bear'd."

Chingu and Shinyuu shot a glance at each other. Drizzle gasped. "Who? Who's that?" Flurry inquired in a softer tone than before.

"You've not heard of Black Bear'd?" asked one of the polar bears with extreme disbelief in his tone.

"No. Should I have?" replied the young cub.

"He's the most ruthless and evil pirate there ever was. He's as ferocious at sea as any other grizzly bear would be on land," replied another of the polar bears.

"Wait ... a grizzly bear? He's a grizzly bear?" Flurry questioned.

"Indeed! His ship, the Arctos, is just off

our port side, and will rendezvous with us at any moment."

"Right!" another prisoner spoke up. "He'll want to claim his prize. Who knows what he'll do with us then."

"Probably taking us to our new home at the bottom of Davy Jones' locker," added another of the polar bear captives. Grumbling broke out among the white-furred brutes, and panic came upon their faces when they discussed their missing crewmembers.

"Let's focus on the moment at hand. We need a plan," Chingu interjected. He turned to who appeared to be the one in charge of the polar bear group. Chingu asked, "How fast is the Arctos? Can it outrun us if we steal this ship?"

"Nobody can outrun Black Bear'd. His

ship will roll right over us if we try to escape. Besides, our captain is aboard that grizzly's ship. We can't run away and leave him behind."

"Cloud?" Shinyuu exclaimed.

"How did you know? Do you know him?" they replied.

"Know him? He's my best friend. That's why we're here. We've been trying to find him for weeks already. We feared he might be dead," Shinyuu explained.

"Dead? No. A slave? Yes. Black Bear'd is trying to recruit volunteers to join some sort of secret army. Anyone who refuses has to face …" There was a sudden silence as the bear looked to and fro, before he whispered, "… The sorcerer."

"So?" Flurry spoke up in a hushed voice. "What's so special about that, and why are you whispering?"

"He's very powerful and might hear us if we speak his name," came the reply.

"Oh, come on! How bad can he be? I mean, we beat Jack Frost! You can't get much worse than that, can you?" Flurry looked at their faces and felt a lump in his throat as he more hesitantly asked, "You can't get worse than Jack, can you?"

"Wait a minute, you defeated Jack Frost?" the polar bear crew inquired.

"Uh huh!" Flurry replied.

"Now, wait a minute! I defeated him," shouted Drizzle.

"We both did. It was a group effort," Flurry responded smugly.

"No, it wasn't! You were down below. I was the one that ran up and tackled him!" Honja looked annoyed. The bunny sat there and shook his head. Caboose looked back and forth between the two bear cubs as they argued.

"Guys!" Boaz tried to intervene. "Guys!" It was no use, they continued to bicker and raise their voices another octave with each exchange. Boaz yelled as loud as he could. "Guys!"

"What?" Flurry and Drizzle shouted in unison. They turned and glared at the plush lion in anger.

"You might want to pay attention to him," Boaz said as he pointed to the door.

Just a few feet away stood one of their pirate captors with a look of disbelief on his face. Before he had a chance to alert the entire crew, Chingu drew his sword and dispatched the intruder.

"Well, that's how we're getting past the

door," Shinyuu spoke with amusement in his words before he got smacked across the back of the head. "Hey!"

"Would you focus and help me drag him out of sight?" Chingu asked, though it sounded more like an order than a question to Shinyuu.

"Allow me to help," offered the leader of the polar bear group. Chingu rushed over with the keys, unlocked the bear's shackles, and then passed the keys on to the others. "My name is Audun, by the way," said the leader of their massive new friends.

"Chingu," replied the red panda. They clasped each other's wrist and shook.

Shinyuu quietly pushed the door shut without letting it latch and peeked through the sliver of space between the door and its frame.

One of the polar bears grabbed the downed pirate's sword, and the others clothed themselves in their decorative attire. Flurry thought the polar bears reminded him of Vikings, with the beautiful knotwork lining their items of clothing.

Shinyuu turned from the door, grabbed his own weapons from where they had been stowed away, and strapped them to his side. His sword was unique. Though it did not have a paw guard, the blade curved outward near the grip in such a way that it would deflect an incoming attack. His upper clothing was white and resembled what Flurry had seen a samurai wear in some of the movies he liked to watch. Shinyuu's lower garment appeared to be a long black skirt of some kind. He looked magnificent.

Drizzle did likewise. Flurry peered at him

with a look jealousy on his face. Flurry realized that Drizzle had a sword but he did not. "What?" Drizzle asked.

"Nothing!" Flurry answered, turned his back to Drizzle, and crossed his arms.

"Whatever!" Drizzle commented and briskly walked over to join Chingu. "So what's going on?" he asked.

Flurry was not to be left out of the loop. He snuck up behind everyone and tried to listen in.

"Well, we need to get to Black Bear'd's ship to free Cloud. Any ideas?" Chingu asked. He looked at Drizzle.

"Me?" Drizzle asked with a start. Chingu nodded.

"Why didn't anyone ask me?" Flurry whispered to his friends. Honja immediately grumbled something in his native tongue, head-butted Flurry, and stormed off in anger.

"Not everything's about you," Boaz replied.

"It should be!" Flurry responded. Then he turned to the other conversation and spoke up. "I think we should take the ship," Flurry commented.

"Sat would be stealing. My mommy said sat is bad," Caboose lisped his two cents' worth of advice.

"Yeah, Caboose, you're right," Boaz addressed his little friend. "However, sometimes we have to do things in order to survive."

"What do you mean?" Caboose asked.

"Never mind that! Why was it wrong to steal food, but now it's okay to steal a ship?" Flurry inquired of Boaz.

"Caboose, don't worry, we aren't stealing this ship. We're going to steal Black Bear'd's ship instead," Drizzle interjected.

"Whoa!" came the response of the polar bears. Their legs nearly buckled at the sound of Drizzle's proposal.

"Oh, okay then," Caboose replied.

Boaz smacked himself in the forehead out of disbelief. Flurry chimed in. "What? You just told me that stealing is wrong, but now it's okay if Drizzle helps steal a different ship?"

"Uh huh!" Caboose answered, though it was clear Caboose had no idea what he was saying or even agreeing to.

"It's like everyone is against me today," Flurry mumbled to himself.

Noah and Boaz chuckled at Flurry's expense. They always enjoyed seeing Flurry frustrated. Honja ignored everyone and kept his distance. He did not want any part of that venture at all.

Meanwhile, the polar bears were still grumbling over Drizzle's proposal. "What you suggest is madness! We can't take Black Bear'd's ship!"

"Yes, we can! I have a plan," Drizzle addressed their skepticism and discussed it in every detail. Chingu had a slight hint of a grin. It was clear that Chingu was pleased with Drizzle's fascinating strategy.

Chingu, Shinyuu, and the polar bear prisoners were eventually won over. Now convinced the plan would work, they readied themselves and made their way out of the door and across the ship's hold.

"So far, so good," said Chingu as he scanned the deck. Thankfully, he did not find anyone around.

They worked their way over to the steps that led to the next deck above. Shinyuu peeked around the corner and gave paw signals to his brother. Slowly and quietly, they worked their way from deck-to-deck, dealing with any opposition they came across.

At last, they were at the threshold of the main deck. Chingu scouted the area visually. When he was about to exit onto the main deck, he turned back and warned, "Flurry, you and the others stay down below. This part is going to be the most dangerous."

"I can stay behind and look after them," Shinyuu replied. Chingu shot him an angry glare, for he knew Shinyuu hated to fight and would make up any excuse to get out of it. "I'm just kidding! I'm coming! I'm coming!" Shinyuu backpedaled.

"I'll walk out first. The rest of you stay here until you're needed. I don't want to tip them off to our numbers unnecessarily." Chingu then walked out onto the main deck.

With calm, cool confidence, Chingu approached the other pirates. Startled at his presence, one of the pirates looked up and shouted, "You there! Stop!"

"Who goes there?" barked another.

"How did he get on our ship?" questioned another crewman, who quickly reached for his sword.

"Who cares? Deal with him!" shouted the captain.

The entire pirate crew drew their swords and ran toward the red panda warrior. Chingu's eyes narrowed. He moved into a fighting stance and slowly reached for his sword. The pirates paused, looked at each other, and then back at Chingu.

They could see the level-headed confidence that permeated the red panda's very being. Unfortunately, none of the pirates were wise enough to fear Chingu. In fact, none of them knew who they were dealing with at all. As far as they were concerned, he was nothing of consequence.

They each let out battle cries and simultaneously swung their razor sharp blades at the red panda, but Chingu was too fast. With a back flip, he leapt into the air and brought down his first opponent.

Chingu quickly turned to the others and engaged them in a heated battle. The sound of metal on metal resounded throughout the ship. Down below, Flurry could not take it anymore. He had to know what was going on. "I'm out of here, guys!" yelled the white bear cub before he sprinted up the steps.

"Wait! Chingu said to stay here!" shouted the others. They chased after him.

Flurry joined Shinyuu, Drizzle, and the polar bears where they all stood and watched Chingu fight everyone by himself. "Hey! Why aren't any of you helping him?" Flurry asked.

"I am helping. Look at the great drawing I made," Shinyuu replied and giggled to himself. He held up a silly sketch of his brother.

Drizzle spun around and knocked the drawing out of Shinyuu's paw. "Hey!" came the red panda's reply.

"This isn't the time for goofing around!" Drizzle shouted at Shinyuu.

Flurry looked out at the deck, and his jaw

dropped at the sight of the battle that raged on. Chingu had improved since Flurry last saw him. In fact, Chingu was even better than Flurry's favorite heroes from the movies he liked to watch.

He dodged kicks, ducked under punches, sidestepped strikes, and matched blades. Chingu dropped his enemies one-by-one.

The red panda warrior whistled to signal the others to join him to deal with the remaining three pirates. The polar bears ran out onto the deck. The remnant of the pirates dropped their swords and raised their paws to the sky.

"We give up!" one of them said.

Another shouted, "We surrender!"

The captain had too much pride to speak, but he knew he had been defeated. He also laid down his weapon and joined the other two.

"Are we going to make them walk the plank?" Flurry asked enthusiastically.

Everyone spun around and glared at him. "I thought I told you to stay below," Chingu shouted.

"Yeah, about that. I ..." Flurry struggled to find an excuse before he continued. "... Forgot? Yeah, that's it! I forgot. Oops! Shame on me!" It was clear he was putting on an act. Nearly everyone shook their head at him. Flurry stood there with his arms behind his back and sported an uneasy grin on his face.

"Leave it to Flurry to not do what he's told," Drizzle replied. Noah, Boaz, Caboose, and Honja all vigorously nodded their heads in adamant agreement.

"Hey!" Flurry shouted.

"You know, he's right," Boaz added.

"Uh huh," Caboose chimed in.

"Oh, great! I see how it is! Everyone's against me, is that it?" Flurry was visibly angry, but it would have to wait. Chingu and Audun looked out at the other two ships. One ship headed off in the opposite direction, but the Arctos approached them.

"What do we do now?" Audun sternly demanded an answer from Chingu.

"We let him come," Chingu replied. He then looked at the others and shouted out commands. "Hurry! We don't have much time. Throw everything off the ship."

"Hey!" bellowed Flurry as Noah, Boaz, Honja, and Drizzle pushed him to the side of the ship.

"Guys, come on!" shouted Chingu. Shinyuu giggled, but it was brought to a halt with another smack to the back of the head from his brother.

"Ouch!" Shinyuu complained and rubbed his head.

"Stop fooling around! Black Bear'd is coming!" Chingu yelled over the busy preparations being made all around them.

Everyone quickly got their act together and ran all over the ship to throw everything overboard, including the pirates, while Chingu had some of the crew prepare the sails to give them the best speed possible. He wanted their plan to be convincing.

Down below, Boaz, Caboose, Honja, Noah, Shinyuu, and Drizzle tossed out cannonballs, barrels, rope, black powder, pitch, hammers, nails, cots, and anything else they could find. The polar bears did the heavier lifting.

As they tossed the cannonballs over the side, Flurry felt concerned. "Hey! Won't we need those to shoot at the bad guys?"

"No. Our plan isn't to fight, but to outrun Black Bear'd. So we need the ship to be lighter," answered Boaz.

"That's not entirely true," Drizzle replied. "Our plan is to make Black Bear'd *think* we're trying to outrun him, when in fact we want him to catch us."

"What?" Flurry exclaimed. "That's the worst idea in the history of bad ideas!"

"Why am I not surprised you'd think that?" Drizzle replied.

"Oh, I don't know! Maybe because it's a terrible idea?" came Flurry's sarcastic retort.

Luckily, Shinyuu was there to back Drizzle up. "Actually, his plan is genius. Black Bear'd will think we're running from him, and he'll try to catch up. Then we sneak onto his ship while his crew boards this one. Before he knows what hit him, we're stealing his ship and leaving him and his crew behind."

"Wow! That's a brave plan," Boaz responded. He was clearly impressed.

"Whatever! I totally could've thought of that, too," Flurry replied.

"Sure, Flurry! Sure!" Boaz answered sarcastically.

Flurry opened his mouth to respond, but before he could defend himself, there was a loud, thundering sound, and then another. "Uh, what was that?

"Cannon fire," Boaz responded.

"We're being fired upon!" shouted Shinyuu.

"I guess we got his attention," Drizzle

answered with his ears covered. Drizzle never could handle loud noise, and he was beginning to wish he was not there.

The cubs all rushed over to the gun ports to peek out. Sure enough, Black Bear'd's ship closed in on them quickly.

Chingu made haste down the steps. "Okay, everyone, it's go time! Let's do this!" He looked over at the polar bears, nodded to them, and said, "You know what to do." The polar bears concurred. "Okay, guys, let's go."

Black Bear'd's ship taxied alongside. The sound of footsteps was heard up above. They were being boarded. The new group of pirates was more fearsome than the previous bunch. Black Bear'd's crew was primarily comprised of grizzly bears, panthers, wolves, and coyotes.

While the ship was being captured, Chingu and the others crawled out through the gun ports. They connected the adjacent cannons with ropes, climbed across, and into the gun ports of Black Bear'd's ship.

Now in the bowels of the villain's vessel, it was time for the next stage in Drizzle's plan.

CHAPTER 3
PLAN B

The Arctos was a massive ship. The imposing shadow it cast enveloped its prey as it closed in on the smaller vessel that only a moment ago attempted to flee. Black Bear'd stepped out from the captain's cabin and addressed his crew. "Bring me the prisoners! Theran has something special planned for them!"

The crew groveled at the sound of his voice. "Yes, sir! Right away, sir!" they all replied.

Black Bear'd was a sight to behold. If being a grizzly bear was not enough to incite fear, the sheer fact that he stood more than eight feet tall would make anyone quake in their boots. However, Black Bear'd took it a step further. The tips of his beard were on fire. Nobody knew how that was possible without catching the rest of his beard or even his clothes on fire, too. His crew assumed he had dabbled in evil powers of some kind to achieve that. With his eyes aglow like burning embers, fearsome was an understatement when Black Bear'd came to mind.

The pirate captain stood on the deck of his ship and observed his crew board the runaway vessel. Little did he know what took place right below his boots.

Flurry and the others had now snuck

aboard the ship. They left the polar bears back on the other ship. That would have seemed like a cowardly thing to do if it was not all part of the plan. Drizzle had explained to him that the polar bear crew would be brought aboard and act as a distraction from their mission to free their friend Björn, also known as Captain White Cloud.

It was Shinyuu who started Cloud's nickname. Björn was a big, white polar bear, and Shinyuu liked to refer to him as a big, white, fluffy cloud.

Flurry agreed with Shinyuu's assessment when they entered the brig and found more polar bear prisoners, along with Björn himself. Flurry now only thought of him as Cloud.

"Cloud!" Shinyuu cheerfully shouted.

"You're alive!" The red panda rushed over to his friend and removed his shackles.

"Shinyuu?" Cloud replied, unsure if his eyes were playing tricks on him or not. "Is that really you?" The polar bear grabbed Shinyuu, picked him up, and gave him a big bear hug. With a boisterous laugh he added, "It's great to see you, old friend!"

After being set back down, Shinyuu gave introductions. "I'm sure you remember my closest brother, Chingu. He's the one you should thank. We couldn't have done it without him."

Chingu bowed, but Cloud approached and grasped the young warrior by the wrist and shook. "I'm honored to be in your presence, again."

"Likewise," Chingu replied.

"And who are these little ones?" Cloud

inquired.

"My name is Drizzle," the black-furred cub spoke up first. "I travel with Chingu." He pointed to the others and continued. "This is Flurry, Noah, Caboose, Boaz, and Honja."

Cloud motioned at the other polar bears and responded, "These are what's left of my crew. This is my quartermaster Einar; the big brute of a bear in the back is Egil; and standing behind all of you is Stian. I wish more of my crew had survived, but sadly we're all that's left." Grief filled Cloud's face when he relayed his words.

"Not true!" Flurry responded. "The others are alive, too."

"What?" Cloud's face lit up.

"Yeah, it's true," Drizzle replied as he shot Flurry a frustrated look. The two of them were always in competition with each other. These were Drizzle's new friends, but Flurry always wanted to be the center of attention and take credit for everything. Flurry had a smug look on his face. With his arms crossed, he stood there and stared back at Drizzle. Drizzle grunted and turned away.

The sound of many footsteps were heard up above, and a sudden commotion. "What's going on?" Cloud asked.

Chingu spoke up. "That's part of our plan. Your crew is being brought aboard as captives. Black Bear'd has no idea we are down here or that you have been freed. When we attack, our full force will be on his ship. He won't know what hit him."

Life came back to the faces of the polar bear captives. They quickly armed themselves. "Bring it on!" exclaimed Egil, the largest and most forbidding of the polar bear team.

Chingu and Shinyuu had already taken care of any enemies below deck before they worked their way to the brig. Their only opposition was up above. As they made their way to the final set of steps, Cloud suddenly froze. He slowly turned to Chingu with a stone-cold expression on his face. "You did make sure 'he' isn't on the ship, right?"

Not understanding the question, Chingu replied, "I'm certain Black Bear'd is on the ship."

"No, not him. I want him here; I have a score to settle. I'm talking about his friend. The evil sorcerer."

"We haven't seen any sign of him," Shinyuu replied.

"Perhaps he's on the other ship?" Drizzle

inquired.

"Let's hope so," Cloud continued. "If he's here, this will all be for nothing."

Flurry swallowed hard. He was not certain who Black Bear'd or the sorcerer were, but by the way they all talked about those two, Flurry imagined the worst.

Chingu looked back at the cubs and said, "Just like last time, all of you stay behind." Chingu inched his way forward, paused, and then turned back and added, "Flurry, I mean it! Stay put this time."

Flurry was incensed with Chingu's statement and shouted, "Me? Why is it always me?" Noah leapt toward Flurry and put his paw over the bear's mouth, but it was too late. Flurry had blown their cover.

A pirate whirled around and pointed at them. "There! We have stowaways aboard!"

Black Bear'd shifted his flaming gaze toward them. Before he could react, Chingu, Shinyuu, Cloud, and the other three polar bears charged with a bellowing battle cry. The rest of the polar bear crewmembers took advantage of the distraction. That was their chance. They broke free from their captors, armed themselves, and a full-out battle ensued.

Flurry and the others watched as swordfights raged on. He felt tense when Cloud and Black Bear'd locked blades. With Cloud's blue coat and Black Bear'd's red coat, it was easy to pick them out from the drab, brown chaos. The captains growled and roared at each other as they traded blows from each other's fists.

Chingu was magnificent with his blade and defended against all incoming attacks.

Shinyuu still had not drawn his sword. In fact, Flurry had not observed Shinyuu take out his blade even once since they met. Shinyuu fought using his paws. He delivered punches, kicks, leg sweeps, arm bars, and grappled his enemies.

Flurry turned to Drizzle and asked, "Have you ever seen Shinyuu use his sword?"

"No. Why?" Drizzle replied.

"Oh, just wondering," Flurry answered.

Flurry, Drizzle, Noah, and Boaz watched the skirmish while Honja remained hidden beneath the bottom step. Caboose was inexplicably absent, yet again. He had a habit of slipping away without anyone ever noticing. When Flurry looked back at his friends, he was dismayed at the absence of his most loyal follower.

"Caboose? Caboose?" He asked the

others, "Have any of you seen Caboose?"

Noah shook his head and shrugged. The others answered, "No."

They scanned the area, but no trace of their plush polar bear could be found. The gang was immediately concerned and jumped to action. They quickly descended the flight of steps and looked around while they called out for their friend. "Caboose! Caboose! Where are you?"

"Oh, dear! I hope he's okay," Drizzle commented with genuine concern.

"He always does this," answered Flurry, equally concerned.

"We need to keep a closer eye on him," Boaz chimed in.

Noah pulled out a pair of binoculars, to indicate he was looking, before he put them back wherever he got them.

"Whoa! Wait a minute! Did you guys just see that?" Boaz asked.

"What?" shouted Flurry and Drizzle in unison.

"Noah!" Boaz replied.

"We're looking for Caboose, silly!" Flurry answered.

"No! I mean, he keeps doing things that should be impossible," Boaz insisted with a frustrated tone of voice.

"What are you talking about?" Drizzle asked. "Are you seeing things?"

"Yeah, I'll have to agree with Drizzle. You're sounding kind of crazy," Flurry added.

"I'm not! I'm not! He had a pair of binoculars, and now he doesn't. Earlier today he had a rifle and a sword, back when we were prisoners. He's been doing this stuff for months now! How's it that none of you ever notice it?"

"Okay, Boaz, you've had your fun. Now can we get back to looking for Caboose?" Flurry attempted to put an end to Boaz's crazy talk.

Boaz sighed and in an irritated tone replied, "Fine!"

The gang continued their hunt while up above the swordfight raged on. The fury between the two crews had grown into an all-consuming fire, filled with roaring, growling, clawing, and smashing.

"Come here, you little ..." shouted a panther. He was Black Bear'd's first mate. The panther grew weary as he chased Shinyuu around the mast. The red panda was too quick. With the enemy's every punch or lunge with the sword, Shinyuu would counter, sidestep, or redirect his opponent. He truly knew paw-to-paw combat unlike any other.

Chingu was light on his feet and danced through his opponents like he was part of a ballet. Now, with his sword split into two halves, he deflected attacks from both sides. He did not even break a sweat as he dealt harshly with his attackers.

White Cloud and Black Bear'd continued to pummel each other. Their deep-seated hatred toward each other was set loose. Cloud had a long-standing hatred for the grizzly bear captain. Black Bear'd murdered Cloud's father long ago. The polar bear had been on a quest for revenge ever since.

The battle was clearly in Chingu and Shinyuu's favor, but for Cloud it was not so clear. At times it appeared that Cloud had the upper hand; at other times, Black Bear'd. One distraction could lead to the other's demise, and that was when Cloud made a mistake. A defeated groan filled the air. One of Cloud's crewmates had fallen by the sword. That split-second distraction allowed Black Bear'd to catch Cloud off guard. The grizzly punched Cloud in the face and swept his leg out from under him. The polar bear captain crashed down to the deck.

Black Bear'd kicked the polar bear's sword away and pointed the tip of his own weapon right in Cloud's face. "Well, this is how it ends," said the fiery-eyed grizzly.

Cloud looked up at his enemy and growled at him in anger. "This isn't over!"

"Oh, but it is!"

"Never!"

"You fail to realize that nobody can beat

me," bragged the evil bear.

"I'll get another chance; mark my words."

"Consider them marked." Black Bear'd raised his sword and prepared to deliver a death blow when his own distraction came.

BOOM! One of Black Bear'd's cannons fired. The evil pirate looked in the direction of the blast. Cloud grabbed Black Bear'd by the hem of his coat and threw him over the side of the ship into the raging waves below.

BOOM! Another cannon fired. Smoke filled the air. The ship shook, and wooden debris flew every which way as the smaller ship was being blown to bits. *BOOM!* "What's going on?" White Cloud shouted.

Down below, the source of the cannon fire was quite evident. "Caboose, Stop! Caboose! Don't do that! Stop!" shouted the others.

Caboose had found a flaming stick. He was fascinated with the way it made sparkles when he touched it to the tiny ropes he kept finding all over the place. He believed it was some kind of light show, and he enjoyed every moment of it. Caboose went around to all of the cannons to see the sparkles. The loud booms were like fireworks to him.

Noah held up an eight-sided red sign with the word STOP on it and waved it back and forth. Boaz glanced over at Noah and did a double-take.

"Where did you get that?" Boaz asked the tall, slender lion. Noah shrugged and acted like he giggled. Boaz climbed up some crates, grabbed one side of the stop sign, and hollered to the others, "Guys! Look! I'm not crazy! Noah has a stop sign! This isn't possible!"

Noah ripped the sign away and stashed it before the others looked. Annoyed, Flurry replied, "Boaz, this isn't the time!" Flurry turned back to Caboose and continued to call out to him.

Boaz flopped down on the crate. He felt discouraged. Boaz looked over and saw Honja, partially hidden behind a distant barrel. "You saw it, didn't you?" Honja nodded his head in agreement. "Finally, somebody who doesn't think I'm crazy," Boaz grunted to himself.

At the sight of Flurry, Caboose hustled toward him. He wanted to show his pal what a great toy he had discovered. As Caboose ran with the stick in his mouth, he inadvertently lit other things on fire.

"Stop, Caboose! Stop!" shouted Flurry

and the others.

"Caboose, put it down!" Drizzle bellowed. He rushed over and stamped out the mini-fires while he kept his paws over his ears – which he had been doing the entire time. Drizzle hated loud noise. In fact, he hated busy environments, too. So his adventure was more than he bargained for. He desperately wanted to hide himself away in a crate or something.

Caboose came to a screeching halt and dropped the piece of wood. "What? It makes sparkles! See, Flurry?"

"Yes, yes, I see it," Flurry quickly responded with obvious anxiety in his tone.

All of them tried to calm down and get their breath back. They were exhausted from their attempt to chase the little fellow down.

Boaz panted heavily. "Guys, remind me

to start exercising if we get out of this alive," said the lion cub.

"Surely nobody noticed that, right? Right?" Flurry asked optimistically.

"Are you kidding me?" Drizzle loudly exclaimed. "Of course they noticed! That ship is sinking as we speak!" Drizzle leaned against the wall, rubbed his head, and groaned. "Man, do I have a headache!"

"I'm sure it'll be fine," Flurry replied uneasily.

"Maybe if I can get away from all of this noise," answered Drizzle.

"Not you! I mean the ship," Flurry responded.

"If by 'fine' you mean sunk beneath the ocean ... then yeah, it'll be fine," came Boaz's sarcastic remark.

"This changes our plans. We can't keep

the prisoners here. What should we do now?" Drizzle asked himself out loud.

Noah ran up to a board, grabbed it, and laid it at an angle against a barrel of gunpowder. He then walked across the plank, acted like he was holding his nose, and jumped off.

"What's he doing?" asked Boaz.

"Swimming!" shouted Caboose. "Can we go swimming?"

"That's it!" Drizzle shouted. "We throw everyone off of the ship!" Drizzle did not waste any time. He ran off faster than anyone could react.

"Seemed fairly obvious to me," Flurry commented.

Boaz shouted, "I swear! It's like I'm not even here!"

In a moment of sarcasm, Flurry turned to

Boaz and said, "What did you see? A shark?" Flurry giggled to himself. Boaz huffed, crossed his arms, and looked away.

On the main deck of the Arctos, the two crews continued to battle. They did not have time to worry about the sinking vessel on the starboard side. Drizzle ran up to Chingu, but one of the coyote pirates swung at him. Drizzle pulled his sword to deflect the incoming blade, and he shouted to his friend. "Chingu, throw them overboard! Let's finish this and steal the ship!"

Chingu smiled and nodded. One-by-one, their enemies went for a swim. In a moment, the ship was theirs.

"Hurray!" shouted Flurry and the gang as they ran out onto the main deck. Honja hid under a fallen pirate hat. He was only willing to peek out from time-to-time.

Everyone took a moment to cheer and exchanged hugs and pawshakes.

Cloud wasted no time taking command of the Arctos. He ordered his crew to set sail, and moments later they were off. The ship sailed out to the open sea.

CHAPTER 4
CLEVER ESCAPE

Black Bear'd held onto the broken mast of the sinking ship and watched the Arctos depart. He had never been bested before, and he was not about to allow White Cloud to get away with it. He had a fearsome reputation, and he would deal harshly with his enemies for having tarnished it.

Back aboard the Arctos, a celebration was underway. The polar bear crew ate of Black Bear'd's food and drank of his beverages while they shared war stories with one another.

Down below, Flurry and the other fuzzies explored. It was a dream come true. Flurry was on his own pirate adventure. "What's behind this door, I wonder?" Flurry asked. He pulled on the corner of the door, but it was no use. He was so tiny that he could not open any of the doors.

Then, true to nature, Caboose ran across the deck wearing a tricorn hat. He ran toward Flurry and shouted, "Look! Look what I found!" Without warning, Caboose slipped on a wet plank and fell flat on his belly. With his legs splayed out to his side, he spun around one-hundred and eighty degrees. Everyone laughed. Caboose sat up and joined in the amusement.

Drizzle removed the hat from Caboose's head. "Where did you get that?" he inquired.

Without a moment's hesitation, Flurry snatched it away. "He was bringing it to show me! It's not yours!" Flurry shouted.

"Here we go again," Boaz muttered to himself and rolled his eyes. Both Noah and Honja nodded in agreement.

"I wasn't going to keep it! I just wanted to look at it!" Drizzle shouted back.

"Nope! Mine!" Flurry hugged the hat close to his chest

"*Babo yah!*" came a comment from Honja in his own language.

"I agree," Boaz replied to the little rabbit.

Of course, Flurry always liked to pretend that he knew everything, so he chimed in, "Yeah, Honja! It is mine! Thank you!"

"That's not what he said," Boaz replied.

"Of course it is!" answered Flurry.

Honja ran over, nipped Flurry on the foot,

and darted off to be alone again.

"Hey! What was that for?" Flurry shouted. Drizzle giggled at Flurry's expense.

Flurry was indignant. "It's not funny!" he shouted. In response, Drizzle laughed louder, which only made Flurry more frustrated. "It's not funny!" the cub shouted.

Drizzle decided to defuse the tension and asked Caboose, "Where did you find the hat?"

"Sis way!" lisped Caboose. He dashed off toward an open door. Noah, Flurry, and Drizzle ran after him while Boaz and Honja stayed behind. They already had their fill of Flurry and desperately needed a break from his presence.

When they entered the room, Flurry and Drizzle's mouths dropped open. The room was filled with gold coins, silver chalices, crowns, jewels, and a chest full of fancy robes and new clothing.

"Wow!" shouted Flurry. "We hit the jackpot!"

Drizzle and Flurry exchanged giddy glances before they leapt into the pile of goodies. Noah rushed over to a rack of clothing and started trying outfits on.

"That's a great idea, Noah!" Flurry shouted and ran over to join him. "We can dress up as pirates."

A great deal of time passed while they tried on various outfits. Flurry had a silly looking vest, a pair of boots, an eye patch, and a red bandana on his head.

Noah came out from behind the rack all decked out. He had a red bandana and a tricorn hat upon his head. He wore boots that went all of the way up to his knees, gray pants, a white shirt, and a vest. He even braided his mane at the sides of his head and below his chin to make it appear as if it was a beard.

When Flurry saw him, he could not contain his laughter. "You look so silly!" Flurry dropped to the floor and laughed. "Pirates don't dress like that!" Flurry pointed at the lion, fell to his back, and continued in his laughter. He kicked his legs back and forth, and he held his gut. His laughter grew beyond his ability to control.

The cheer was infectious. Before long they were all caught up in the merriment. The lion toned his garb down and decided to just go with a smaller pair of boots, an eye patch, and the hat.

Flurry did likewise with his own wardrobe choices. He ditched the vest and his eye patch. When he tossed the eye patch to the ground, Caboose rushed over and put it on. Anything Flurry touched was like gold to Caboose. The plush polar bear looked up to and respected Flurry a great deal. He wanted to be just like Flurry. So it made sense that Caboose also put on Flurry's discarded bandana.

Now dressed in a pair of boots and a hat, Flurry was ready to be a pirate.

Drizzle found no need for any of it; he had grown up a lot since he and Flurry last met. Drizzle had not told Flurry or the others, but he had not been home in an exceptionally long time. He had begun a new life on the road with Chingu. However, the saddest part to that story was that his parents back in Ursus did not miss him or even care that he was absent.

As they were about to leave, something else caught Flurry's eye. "Oooh!" he exclaimed and ran over to pick up a gold statue of what appeared to be a weasel. At least that was what Flurry assumed it to be; the figure was actually an ermine. "Wow! This is so cool! It's so cute, but not as cute as me, though. I think I'll put it on my nightstand back home."

At the sound of Flurry's comment, the countenances of his brothers fell. In the heat of the moment, they had forgotten all about the fact that they still had no idea where they were or how to get back home.

"I miss Mommy," said Caboose in a sad voice.

"Yeah, me, too," Flurry answered. Noah nodded in agreement.

"Well, we've finished our mission.

Chingu and I found Shinyuu. Then Shinyuu found Cloud. Together we defeated Black Bear'd, and now we have a ship. I see no reason why they can't help all of you to get back home," Drizzle reasoned.

However, his deduction could not be further from the truth. Up above, Chingu, Shinyuu, and Cloud met together in the captain's cabin.

"It's not that I'm ungrateful. I appreciate what you've done for me, but I can't move on without finding the rest my crew," Cloud explained to the red pandas.

Cloud got up and paced back and forth. His speech continued. "You see, if these few shipmates survived, then there's a chance that other members of my crew survived, too. All I need is a few days to sail to Amur. It's the nearest port city in the Panmeare

Province.

"After Black Bear'd burned my ship to ash, I feared we would all be lost at sea. Some of us were captured, some died, and others are still unaccounted for.

"Besides, going to Amur is mutually beneficial. I have plenty of resources there. I can get you provisions for your trip home, and maybe even find you another ship. Or find myself a new ship and give you this one."

"Sounds good to me. I could use some time off," Shinyuu answered.

Chingu was in deep thought before he looked up and nodded with approval.

"Very well then, to Amur we go," were the captain's closing words.

The three adjourned and exited the captain's cabin to be met by an entourage of little furry cubs that ran toward them.

"Can we go home now?" they all asked with one voice.

Chingu nodded and said, "We're headed to the port city of Amur. We'll get another mode of transportation back to Tigris. From there, we'll take all of you back to Ursus."

"Yay!" they all shouted and jumped up and down.

Nightfall snuck up on them. The moon shone brightly, and the stars sparkled like diamonds. The reflection of the various lights in the sky shimmered in the ocean waves. Chingu stood at the bow of the ship and took it all in. It was his moment to relax, while Flurry and the others played as pirates with their little makeshift swords made from scraps of wood they found throughout the ship.

As Chingu watched the ship cut through the waves, Shinyuu approached. "Orange?" Shinyuu asked. He offered a slice of fruit to his brother.

"Thanks!" Chingu replied.

"I just wanted to thank you again. If not for you, I'd probably be fish food."

Chingu reached over with his free paw and placed it on Shinyuu's shoulder. "No problem. We're family. That's what brothers are for."

"You know what else brothers are good for?"

Chingu knew that Shinyuu was up to something, based on how he had worded his question. Chingu decided to play along and asked, "No. What?"

In an instant, Shinyuu shouted, "Now!" Drizzle came out from hiding and threw a bucket of water toward Chingu. The red panda acted quickly. He grabbed Shinyuu's lapel and yanked him right in the way of the water to shield himself.

Drizzle and Chingu laughed as Shinyuu stood there, sopping wet. "Well, that's what you get when you try to best me. When will you ever learn, dear brother?" Chingu lightly slapped Shinyuu on the back, ate his orange slice, and walked off.

Drizzle continued to point and giggle at Shinyuu. Then the red panda's face lit up. "I know! Let's pull a prank on your friends!" Without a moment's hesitation, Drizzle and Shinyuu rushed off to begin plotting.

It was not long before Flurry and his friends found themselves struggling to stay awake. They all decided to get some shut eye and call it a night.

The next morning came abruptly for Flurry. The cub was sound asleep. He was dreaming about delicious treats and being admired for his cuteness when a bucket of sea water hit him in the face. "Ahhh!" he screamed and jumped to his feet. After he wiped the excess water from his face, Flurry looked up and saw Shinyuu standing there with an empty pail, giggling. "Shinyuu!" Flurry shouted and chased the red panda across the deck.

The others were roused suddenly, due to the chaos that had just ensued. As Boaz, Caboose, and Honja looked around, they saw that Noah had already been awake for a while. He held a wooden staff and followed along as Chingu taught him some new self-defense moves.

Flurry stopped chasing Shinyuu and

looked over to watch Noah and Chingu train together. Many of the polar bears also stood by and looked on.

Flurry recalled how Chingu had trained Noah with vital Yujin Do skills during their last adventure together. He and Drizzle were both immensely grateful that Chingu had done so. They had narrowly escaped the jaws of a ferocious polar bear. Thankfully, Noah intervened at just the right time with some of his newly learned moves.

Sadly, their training was cut short at the sound of Cloud's voice. "Chingu! Come quickly!"

Chingu and Noah bowed to each other, and then the red panda rushed up to meet the captain.

Cloud stood and looked out behind the ship with a brass scope. "Here, take a look," the polar bear insisted as he handed the telescope to Chingu.

Chingu took it and gazed out at the horizon. Off in the distance was another vessel. They were being followed. "Well?" Chingu asked.

"It's too far away to know for sure, but my gut tells me it's Black Bear'd."

"What makes you so sure?"

"I'm willing to bet the third ship came to investigate after they heard all of the cannon fire. They probably found Black Bear'd and his crew adrift, and now they're coming for us."

"We had a head start, and our ship is faster than theirs. How can they be gaining on us?"

"They can't. It should be impossible, unless …" Horror came over Cloud's face.

He cautiously looked around and then back at the red panda. He whispered, "Unless 'he's' there. He could be using his evil powers to speed up their pursuit."

Chingu rushed over to the table that sat back behind the wheel of the ship and unrolled a map. "There!" Chingu pointed to a river. "That's a very large river, and we aren't far from it. Take the ship in there."

"Are you mad? We'll be boxed in. They'll capture us for sure." Cloud's concern was evident.

"We can travel on foot to Amur. The jungle will give us adequate cover. We'll have the advantage there. As for the ship, we'll use it as a decoy while we make our escape."

"I don't like this plan, but we have to make a stand at some point, whether at sea or on land. Quite frankly, I'd like to avoid 'him' at all costs."

"I'll inform my brother. Make the preparations," Chingu instructed Cloud. The red panda descended the steps in search of Shinyuu.

When Chingu reached the last step, he noticed it looked shinier than the others, so he stepped over it. "Awww! I thought I had you that time," came the voice of his brother.

"Shinyuu, this isn't the time or place for practical jokes. We're about to be in another battle. Black Bear'd's back!" Chingu walked off after his announcement.

Shinyuu stood there and felt frightened at the thought of Black Bear'd on their tail. Suddenly there was a loud crash, and the voice of Cloud shouted, "Shinyuu!"

The red panda was certain that Cloud had just slipped on the step meant for Chingu, but he was not going to stick around to find out. He hastily ran down to the deck below to find Drizzle and the others.

Black Bear'd looked out ahead through his scope. In the distance he could see his stolen ship. Rage surged through his veins. He gripped the telescope so tightly that it buckled under the strength of his massive paws.

"You know, we might still need that. I'd appreciate it if you didn't crush it like you did the last one," came the voice of a five-foot tall snow leopard in a purple robe.

The white-furred feline with piercing blue eyes had a crooked grin on his face when Black Bear'd turned and glared at him. They were allies, but it was clear they did not like each other one bit. The grizzly bear slammed the scope down on Theran's paw, eliciting a hiss, and stormed over to the ship's wheel.

The captain shoved the helmsman aside and shouted back at the evil sorcerer. "Can't you get us there any faster?"

Annoyed with all of Black Bear'd's questions, Theran responded with a sigh. "I 'could', but I don't want to drain all of my powers. I need to make sure I'm ready for any surprises they might have for us."

"You worry too much. I'll crush them like the ants they are!"

"Temper, temper!" the snow leopard replied. "You're too hasty. Have patience. We'll both have what we want soon enough."

"Easy for you to say. My crew and I are

the ones doing all of the work," came the snarky reply.

"Enough!" shouted Theran. He slammed his golden staff against the deck floor. He then turned to the helmsman, whispered a single word, and the bear turned to solid ice.

"You think yourself funny, do you?" Black Bear'd marched over and gripped Theran by the throat. "I'd like to see you cast your spells when you're unable to speak. All I have to do is squeeze. Now, free him!"

Black Bear'd released Theran's throat. The sorcerer collapsed to his knees and gasped for breath.

Theran got his senses back and stood up straight. He muttered something, and the other crewmember was freed from the ice. "Our master isn't going to like it when he finds out what you did."

"I don't care. I don't answer to you!"

"You're lucky he wants you alive, or I would end this right here."

Black Bear'd turned to Theran and with an evil grin replied, "No. You're lucky he wants you alive, or you would've been dealt with long ago." Then the grizzly shouted, "Get out of my sight until I call for you!"

Theran quickly rushed off. He huffed and muttered to himself in anger.

Black Bear'd turned to the helmsman and ordered, "Take over! Inform me the moment we catch up with the Arctos!"

"Aye, sir!"

Back aboard the Arctos, a horn sounded loudly. Captain White Cloud was about to make his announcement to prepare for battle. Shinyuu and Chingu stood on each side of him as he manned the wheel. Einar, Cloud's quartermaster, kept watch from the crow's nest up above. He, too, had a horn, and would blow it in different ways to communicate various messages to the crew.

Flurry, Drizzle, and the other plush animals were now outside the captain's cabin at the base of the stairs. "What's going on?" Flurry whispered to Drizzle.

"Black Bear'd is near," came the teddy bear's reply.

Honja shook. Boaz put his arm around the little bunny to comfort him.

BOOM! A distant cannon sounded. Seconds later a cannonball splashed into the ocean just off their starboard bow.

"It's a warning shot," Audun informed the little ones. He ascended the steps to get a look with his telescope. "They're still many leagues off. We'll make it up the river before they catch up to us."

"Good," replied the captain. "Being that far away, their cannons shouldn't be able to reach us. Theran has to be using sorcery!"

The Arctos entered the mouth of the massive river. The water could have accommodated fifty ships side-by-side across its breadth. The captain had one of his crewmates take the helm as he scouted for a place to disembark.

"There! That spot over there has a clearing. We have enough time to drop anchor and get into the forest before they catch up." Cloud slapped the telescope shut and handed it to Audun before he descended the steps.

Chingu turned to Shinyuu. "Get everyone ready to go. We have to make this quick."

Shinyuu bowed to his brother and rushed off.

Flurry and the others were already prepared to go before Shinyuu came down the steps. Most of the gang did not have much, if anything, to pack. Flurry had stashed the golden statue in his pouch. He still took good care of the leather bag he had slung over his shoulder. It was given to him by the elves from Flurry's last adventure. Luckily for him, it was wrapped around his bedpost the morning he found himself and his brothers adrift at sea.

Before they were near enough to the riverbank to abandon ship, something strange took place. "There!" shouted Stian, standing at the bow of the ship.

Audun extended the scope and took a look. What he saw defied logic. Up ahead of them, the water began to freeze into solid ice. To make matters worse, there was another ship that closed in on them from further up the river. "This doesn't look good," Audun informed Chingu and the others within earshot.

Audun blew his horn to get Cloud's attention. Cloud rushed back up the steps. "What is it?"

"We have trouble! Look for yourself," Audun replied.

Cloud peered out and beheld the same sight. The water was freezing over. The ice drew nearer by the second. In a matter of moments they would be stuck in a frozen river.

Drizzle rushed up to find out what the fuss was about. "Go away, cub. This doesn't concern you," Cloud ordered.

"Actually, it does," Chingu spoke in Drizzle's defense. Chingu grabbed the scope and gave it to Drizzle.

"Wow!" Drizzle replied. "How's this possible?"

"I'll tell you how. Theran the sorcerer is aboard that ship, too. This is looking bleak. It was bad enough with Black Bear'd, but both of them?"

"I have an idea!" shouted Drizzle.

"Come on! This isn't the time for games," Cloud dismissed him gruffly.

"Please show some respect," Chingu interjected. "Drizzle is a master strategist. He's the one who formulated the plan to save you and your crew."

"Did he now?" Cloud seemed pleased. "Then by all means, tell me your plan."

"The ice is coming fast! We only have a

few moments before we get stuck. I say we drop the anchor and cut the ship hard to port. It will quickly turn the ship sideways just as we hit the ice. Then some crew members can stay behind and fire off the cannons at the incoming ship while we make our escape. The Arctos would act as a shield from incoming fire and mask our escape across the ice. If we're lucky, they may not fire on us at all, if Black Bear'd doesn't want his ship to be harmed."

Chingu was impressed. He smiled and looked up at Cloud to deduce what the polar bear thought. Cloud was taken aback. He was astounded at such brilliance from a cub so young. He nodded with approval. "It's a brave plan. I like it!" the captain responded. He shouted to his crew, "All hands, prepare to drop anchor on my command!"

The crew readied for action. Cloud spun the wheel and turned the ship sharply to port. He shouted, "Now!"

The ship banked hard and came to a sudden halt when it hit ice. The Arctos had turned ninety degrees just before coming into contact with the frozen water.

"Man the cannons! Fire at will!"

"Aye!" shouted the crew. *BOOM! BOOM! BOOM!* The cannons blasted fire and iron out toward the enemy ship as the rest of the crew climbed down the opposite side of the Arctos by rope and onto the solid ice below.

Before they put their plan into motion, Cloud had spoken privately with his crew. Two of the polar bears volunteered to stay behind to man the guns so the others could escape.

Cloud and his crew were the last to descend from the wooden beast. The captain looked down at the ice. "It's Theran all right. Only he could do this with those evil powers of his," Cloud claimed as he tapped on the ice with his boot.

Flurry and the others were now down safely, minus the two polar bears who opted to stay behind to grant them cover.

"So, what now?" Flurry asked. "We have a ship coming to get us from the ocean, a ship coming down the river, and nothing but ice until we get to land."

"I wish there were a faster way to get across," Boaz chimed in.

"Maybe there is!" Drizzle interjected. "Boaz, come here." The lion obliged and came to Drizzle's side. "With the wood and other supplies aboard, can you make something that would act as a slingshot?"

"Hmmm, I suppose I could," replied the lion.

"Then get to it. That's going to be our escape."

"Care to fill me in on the plan?" Flurry asked.

"Nope!" Drizzle replied with a grin.

The polar bears carried out Drizzle's plan. They lowered different supplies down from the ship, per Boaz's request.

Flurry was so frustrated that he was not the one coming up with all of the brilliant ideas. After all, it was 'his' adventure.

The polar bears worked quickly to construct their makeshift catapult. "Okay, who's first?" asked the captain.

"I volunteer ..." Chingu began, paused, and then added, "Shinyuu!" Shinyuu jerked his head up with a startled expression on his face. Chingu grabbed his brother and put him against the device. The polar bears then launched the red panda up into the air.

Chingu watched as his brother tumbled through the air. He could not help but chuckle a little bit and said, "I always knew he could fly."

"That's not how it's supposed to work," Drizzle chimed in. "I hope he's okay." He turned to the polar bears and said, "Angle it in a way that it slides us across the ice. We'll glide over the surface." Then with a glance back at Chingu, he added, "Hopefully not fly through the air."

"I'm next!" Flurry shouted and ran to the device. Flurry wanted to prove his bravery, as well as experience how fun he imagined it to be.

The cannons continued to fire. Drizzle realized that their time was limited. He shouted, "No time to take turns! We all need to go at once!"

Drizzle grabbed some rope and joined Flurry, Noah, Caboose, Boaz, and Honja. They all held tightly to each other as the polar bears launched them out across the smooth, cold surface of the frozen water.

Away they went! They shot across the ice like bullets. "Weee!" shouted Flurry and Caboose while they glided at breakneck speed. Honja slid on his belly and kept his eyes covered to avoid seeing the horrors of his nightmare of a ride. Boaz and Noah took it in stride.

Chingu was next. He nodded, and off he went. He slid on his back with his feet facing toward his destination.

Up ahead, the other ship had sent over many pirates in longboats to catch Flurry and the others on the ice.

The continuous sound of cannon fire roared on as Cloud's crew attempted to keep Black Bear'd and Theran at bay, but the enemy ship grew closer by the minute.

The new batch of pirates now closed in on them from across the ice. The crooks had no idea what they were in for. A high-pitched squeal came from above. It sounded almost like a scream. One of the pirates looked up just as a red panda landed right on him and punched him in the face.

The pirate fell to the ice. Shinyuu leapt from the first pirate to another target and struck him, too. It was difficult for him to keep his footing, but Shinyuu did well enough. By the time his momentum slowed, he had managed to take down a fair number of their adversaries.

Before long, a barrage of little balls of fur slid under the legs of their would-be captors. As they approached the enemy, Flurry had his first idea. "Drizzle! Throw me the other end of that rope!" he shouted.

Drizzle did as requested. Before long, the pirates found themselves tripped and tangled by Flurry and Drizzle's rope while the cubs speedily coasted under their enemies and on out past them.

Flurry and his friends moved at such speed that the pirates were unable to grab any of them, but Flurry certainly succeeded in knocking a few of them down along the way as he sped past.

"Great, now how are we going to catch them?" grumbled the leader of his pirate brigade.

"Well, at least that wasn't as bad as it could've been," said one of the beat-up pirates as he attempted to get back on his feet.

Then one of them shouted, "Look out!"

The ruffian quickly turned and saw Chingu sliding across the ice toward him. The pirate pulled his sword, but he did not react quickly enough. Chingu pushed off from the ice and leapt into the air. The red panda landed right on the pirate's chest, which knocked the pirate to his back. The momentum caused his body to slide across the ice at only a slightly reduced rate of Chingu's incoming velocity. It was as though Chingu was surfing, and the pirate was his surfboard.

The other pirates drew their swords.

Chingu took out as many as he could until he slid to a stop. The red panda warrior stepped down onto the ice and immediately clashed swords with the enemy. With a stroke here and a swing there, the pirates fell to Chingu or vanished through holes in the ice made by the red panda's blade. When the pirates were about to give up, the polar bears arrived to mop up what was left.

Everyone quickly boarded the longboats that sat at the edge of the ice and rowed to the ship. The enemy vessel floated a safe distance from the frozen part of the river. Chingu and Shinyuu swam to the far side of the ship to ambush what crew remained on deck.

The battle was swift and concise. The red panda brothers dealt with their enemies quickly. At last, the new ship was theirs.

When Cloud and the others boarded, he said, "Drizzle is quite the strategist indeed! He's helped steal three ships already. I may have to make him a member of my crew when I get a ship of my own."

Flurry overheard the comment, flopped down on the floor, and pouted. He did not like Drizzle to get the credit. Flurry's pride issue still had not been attended to, as Christopher Kringle requested of the cub nearly nine months ago.

Cloud's crew quickly readied the ship for departure. They were off before Black Bear'd and Theran arrived.

Back on the enemy vessel, Black Bear'd was livid. "How could you let this happen?" the grizzly shouted at Theran.

"It's not my fault!" the snow leopard shouted back.

"You're the one that decided to turn the river into ice, instead of just speeding up our travel time, like I told you to!"

"I thought the ice would trap them there!"

"You just handed them another ship and enabled them to escape! If you were my crew, I'd have you ..."

"You'd have me what?" Theran stood right in Black Bear'd's face. "Watch what you say. You may not fear me, but I know you fear our master."

Black Bear'd slammed his fist on the rail. "At least we recovered my ship. I'll be glad to be rid of you. Stay here! I'll deal with them myself. They're clearly headed to Amur. Take your ship on up the river. I'll circle around by sea and bombard the city with cannons. No one will escape!"

CHAPTER 5
BRYNJAR

Rays from the setting sun had begun to blanket the landscape. Black Bear'd and Theran's ship was now close enough to board the Arctos.

Black Bear'd's crew transferred to their ship and made preparations to set sail. By that point the ice had begun to melt. However, it would still take a couple of hours to thaw enough to pass through, which would significantly delay Theran from catching up with Cloud and his crew further down the river.

Not fond of setbacks, Theran ordered his crew to take to the ice and chip away at it. Amused, Black Bear'd commented, "What now? You can't use one of your spells to melt it off? Ha, ha, ha, ha, ha!"

Fury filled Theran's face. His eyebrows twitched and his chin quivered. *If not for my master's orders, I'd exact vengeance on that slimy excuse for a bear*, Theran bore in mind. He was a powerful sorcerer, but his powers always came with a cost, and he was not able to use them endlessly. Black Bear'd viewed it as a weakness and scoffed. The grizzly bear and his crew boarded the Arctos and set sail for Amur.

Back aboard Cloud's stolen vessel, the mood grew warmer as they approached the shoreline. "There!" shouted Audun.

"Land ho!" bellowed the other shipmates.

"Weigh anchor!" commanded the captain.

"Aye!" came the response.

"Ready the longboats!" Einar announced. The deck was alive and full of activity. The crew went about their preparations.

Down below, Drizzle made special preparations of his own. "What are you doing?" Boaz inquired.

"Thinking," replied the black-colored bear cub. He paced to and fro. His lips silently mimicked the dialogue in his mind.

"About what?"

"I'm trying to calculate how long it will take for Theran to arrive."

"Oh, that's easy!" Boaz climbed up on a barrel and looked out through one of the gun ports. He peered out in the direction they came. He turned back and asked, "Do you have a telescope?"

"Sure!" Flurry replied, rushed up to the lion, and handed it to him. He had been standing only a few feet away. Unbeknownst to them, he had stuffed his pouch with food and other items he figured he needed. One of said items was a telescope. Flurry thought it would look great in his room back home.

"Thanks?" the lion answered and reached out for the scope. He was hesitant due to Flurry's eagerness to help. He knew Flurry too well to assume he had done it without expecting something in return.

The little lion looked out at the sea. He could see the enemy ship as it approached. He tucked his head back inside, sat down, and held his chin while he calculated.

"What are you doing?" Flurry asked.

"Shhhhh! Let him think," Drizzle interjected.

"I am! Not everyone gets distracted by every little thing like you do!"

"Guys!" Boaz shouted. "Both of you be quiet!" Boaz spent a few more minutes in thought and then scribbled some numbers on the side of a barrel with a piece of coal.

"Okay, I think I've got it. I made some calculations based on where they were and where they are now, and I compared it to our own travel time. I estimate their arrival to be about thirty minutes."

Drizzle took a moment for himself and analyzed the information. Then something caught his attention. Flurry's pack had some sticks of incense that stuck out from under the closed leather flap. "Perfect!" he shouted and snagged them from Flurry's bag.

"Hey! Those are mine! I found them!" Flurry cried out and tried to reclaim his stolen property from Drizzle.

Noah rushed in and pushed the two of them apart. "What's going on?" asked Chingu as he came down the steps.

"He took my incense that I found in the captain's cabin! It belongs to me!" Flurry expounded his side of the story.

Chingu looked to Drizzle for a response. "Yep! That's mostly true!"

"Mostly?" Flurry exclaimed.

"Well, it's true I took them from you. It's not true that they belong to you. You stole them from the captain's cabin, as you said!"

"Chingu! Make him give them back!" whined the white bear cub.

"No! I have a plan that might save us from Theran."

"Oh …" Flurry replied. "Well, why didn't you just say that?"

"I know better than to waste intelligent ideas on you," came Drizzle's jab at Flurry's pride.

"Hey! That's uncalled for!" Flurry turned to Boaz and asked, "What's an in-intuh-intuhgent?"

Boaz shook his head and replied, "Oh, Flurry. You're only proving him right. Can't you just keep your mouth shut for once?"

"No, he always has to have the last word," Drizzle claimed.

"That's not true!" Flurry retorted.

"See! Told you so!"

"Not true!"

"You did it again."

"No, I didn't."

"Guys! Stop it!" shouted the lion cub.

"Instead of fighting, why don't we hear Drizzle's plan?" Boaz looked down at Honja, who stood off at a distance. They exchanged glances to indicate how annoyed they both were with Flurry.

Then under his breath, Honja said, "*Babo yah!*"

"Exactly, Honja! I don't always need the last word," Flurry chimed in again.

"Flurry!" everyone shouted in unison.

"Oh, sorry," he replied. The plush cubs all shot angry glances at him for having to speak last, yet again. Flurry stood there with his arms behind his back and let out an uneasy giggle. Chingu had remained and watched in disbelief while they tried to settle their disagreements.

Drizzle spoke back up. "Okay. My plan is to light the incense. It will act as a time delay on lighting a fuse to one of the cannons. If we extend the wicks, join them together, and calculate the time it takes them to burn, we could possibly time the cannons to fire when Theran's ship arrives. We'll all be long gone. He'll think he's safe, and then …"

"KAPLOOEE!" shouted Flurry. Everyone shot him another angry look. "Okay, I'm going to be quiet now." Then with a motion over his mouth, he indicated that he was zipping his lips.

"I like it," Chingu answered. "Make it so."

When Chingu walked off, Drizzle shouted, "Shinyuu, would you help us angle the cannons so they face in a direction that will hit Theran's ship?" There was nothing but silence for a reply. Drizzle called out again, "Shinyuu?" After another moment of stillness, Drizzle yelled. "Shinyuu! I know you're back there!"

Suddenly, the red panda stumbled out from behind some barrels of gunpowder. "Awww! I was going to jump out and scare all of you. How did you know I was there?"

"How about this? When are you not planning to play a practical joke on someone?" Drizzle answered.

Flurry giggled. "Good one, Driz! Good one!"

Shinyuu stood there and pondered the question for a moment. He looked like he was about to speak up when a shout came from above. "To the longboats!"

Everyone quickly rushed off. Drizzle, Shinyuu, and Boaz stayed to set their trap.

"Good!" Drizzle remarked. "Now that

Flurry's out of my way, I can finally focus." Drizzle bent down and unspooled some wick for the cannons when his face lit up. "Ah ha! I have a great idea! Let's rig two traps. The cannons may not be timed accurately. However, I can prepare something else that will be sure to do the trick." Boaz and Shinyuu nodded with approval, and the three of them got to work.

Back on Theran's ship, their foes were oblivious of the trap they were about to sail right into. The sun was now barely visible over the horizon, and it was apparent that the ship they had now closed in on was abandoned. Cloud, Chingu, Flurry, and all of the others had already made it off of the ship and were on their trek into the heart of the forest.

Theran ordered the ship alongside their

quarry while the crew prepared to board it. They had only been anchored for a few moments when … *BOOM!* The ship shook as a cannonball smashed through the hull.

The suddenness of the entire thing took Theran and his crew by surprise. However, he barely had any time to realize what had happened before he heard, *BOOM! BOOM! BOOM! BOOM! BOOM!*

Multiple cannons fired in succession and blew his ship to bits. The crew abandoned the vessel. They leapt over the side and into the cold water below.

Theran and his crew held on to debris and watched helplessly as their ship sank before their very eyes. Theran was furious. "When I catch them, there'll be no end to the suffering I'll subject them to!"

"At least we can board the other ship,"

came one of his crewmates commented. "I mean, it could've been worse." At that exact moment there was a massive and terrifying *KABOOOM!* The entire ship exploded in a giant ball of fire, which left nothing but fragments of burning wood that rained down all around them.

"I have had enough!" shouted Theran. Using his dark powers, he rose up out of the water and floated through the air to the shore. With a word, he was instantly dry. He then waved his paw, and the entire crew were whisked from the water and planted safely on dry ground.

Theran stormed toward the crewmember who had unwisely spoken moments before. "You! Come here!"

The sailor trembled and slowly inched forward. Cloud and the others had made

Theran look like a fool, but those who knew him were keenly aware of how evil and fearsome he was.

The snow leopard towered over the coyote pirate. Theran was out of patience and grew tired of the mate's slow approach.

The sorcerer reached out with his paw, snagged the coyote with an invisible grip, and dragged the pirate over the remaining distance. Theran touched his staff to the coyote's snout and said, "There! That's for your unwarranted opinion!" The pirate was now unable to speak.

Theran turned to the others and addressed his sopping wet crew. "Does anyone else have anything stupid they would like to say?" Everyone shook their heads vigorously to indicate they were fine with keeping quiet. "Good! On to Amur! Be quick about it! We have an enemy to catch!"

Flurry and the others were well on their way. They speedily ran through the forest. None of Flurry's friends liked being in such a dark and foreboding place. Thankfully, they each had a little lantern to light their steps, but they still could not see what was beyond the foliage just a few feet away.

Honja was the most frightened of all. He already had a timid personality, but being a bunny only compounded his insecurity. Noah stepped in, picked the little rabbit up, and carried him. Honja hated to be touched, but in moments like this, he really needed to be reassured that everything would be okay.

Boaz convinced Caboose to let him ride on his back. Flurry and Drizzle walked side-by-side. Shinyuu was behind them, supposedly to keep an eye out for danger, though Flurry and Drizzle both suspected he was up to something. Chingu and Cloud led the way, with the rest of the polar bear crew dispersed throughout the group.

They walked for hours. Flurry's legs were so tired that he could not go much further. Luckily for him, they arrived at a small town where they could rest.

"Is this Amur? It doesn't look like it to me," Drizzle stated.

"No," answered Chingu. "It's probably three or four more hours away."

"Three more hours!" shouted Flurry.

"Shhhhh!" came the response of the others.

Flurry reiterated with a whisper, "Three more hours? I can't walk another step!"

The group made their way toward the town market. Chingu stood still and looked out at the forest. "What is it?" Drizzle asked just as Shinyuu caught up to them.

"I've been thinking," Chingu replied. "As long as it's been taking us, I'm certain Black Bear'd will reach Amur before we do."

"He's behind us, isn't he?" Shinyuu asked.

"He could be, but it would be a better strategy to flank us," Chingu replied. "Theran could be closing in from behind, while Black Bear'd sails around and catches up to us there."

"So what does this mean?" Drizzle inquired.

"It means that we shouldn't go to Amur," Chingu responded. "We need to change our plan."

Before Chingu could continue, Shinyuu nudged him. He saw Flurry and the others motion for them to follow. The trio caught up with the others outside a pub. "What are we doing here?" Shinyuu asked.

"It turns out, Cloud knew somebody sitting at one of the tables. They're talking now," Flurry replied.

Inside, the pub was full of rowdy characters. It reminded Flurry of Cliffside Peak. The place crawled with mercenaries, pirates, bounty hunters, and every other variety of scum or law breakers you could think of. The tavern was full of life due to the boisterous nature of the patrons.

Cloud sat across a table from a tiger with light-colored fur that looked like a mix between gray and blue. The tiger wore a leather jacket and had a patch over his right eye. The two leaned inward, and spoke in whispers. "I hear you have a ship for hire,"

Cloud inquired.

"Maybe. It depends on who might be asking."

"We've met before. I thought you'd remember me. I'm Captain White Cloud. I'm sure you've heard of my ship, the Mjölnir."

"Heard of it? Of course I have! You're a legend in these parts."

Cloud felt relieved; it seemed as if he had made a connection. Then the tiger's face turned sour and his tone changed. "In fact, if my sources be correct, it was burned to a crisp." Then rhetorically he asked, "And who did that?" With sarcasm he answered his own question, "That's right! Black Bear'd!"

Cloud slammed his fist on the table and grabbed the tiger by the leather belt across his chest. Cloud leaned in closer. "There's no need to point out the obvious. That should have no bearing on my request."

The tiger snapped his fingers, and ten other bar patrons stood up, pulled their swords, and pointed them right at Cloud's head. Cloud's crew drew their own swords, in response to the threat. The tavern was dead silent. Flurry and his friends watched a bad situation that was about to get much worse.

The striped cat laughed and motioned to the others to stand down. Flurry and Drizzle shot each other a confused glance. The tiger's defenders all sat back down. Cloud nodded to his crew that everything was fine, so the polar bears stowed their weapons.

"You've still got that spark, don't you?"

"So, you do remember me!" Cloud stated.

Cloud seemed a bit perplexed as to the tiger's continued laughter and asked, "Is this some kind of joke, or a test?"

"Of course!" replied the tiger.

"Well? Which is it?" the captain asked.

"Take your pick," came a sarcastic reply. "Black Bear'd has spies everywhere. I also had to be sure you hadn't also been …" There was a brief pause. The cat scanned the room and then resumed. "… Turned."

"Turned?" replied White Cloud.

"Yes. Like the rest of your crew."

"They're standing right there. I've noticed nothing wrong with them."

"No, you fool! Not them! The others!"

"Others? What others? I don't follow."

"Theran! Need I really say more?"

"Unfortunately, yes."

With a sigh, he continued. "I see I'm

going to have to practically spell everything out for you. His left paw! It bears a ring. When he places it in front of your eyes, you just aren't the same anymore. Your mind is now shaped to his will. He has done this to many of my own crew, as well as yours."

"How can this be?" Cloud responded.

"You know the evil that flows through him. Besides, it's not just him. There are always the rumors, too."

"What kind of rumors?"

"Rumors that he doesn't work alone."

"We're aware of that. He's in league with Black Bear'd." Cloud's response was met with boisterous laughter.

"Ha, ha, ha, ha, ha! Really? That's what you think? You really don't know, do you?"

Cloud slammed his fist on the table in anger. "Okay, enough with the subterfuge!

Speak plainly! I don't have all day," shouted the polar bear.

"I'll sum it up for you with two words. Jack Frost!"

Cloud's face turned cold at the sound of that name. Flurry and Drizzle gasped and traded concerned glances. The conversation now had Chingu's full attention. He had certainly heard the rumors, but he did not take them too seriously. Chingu thought the tiger might finally provide some insight into the matter.

The red panda rushed over to the table. "That can't be true! It just can't! I watched him die! I was right there!"

"Did he?" asked the tiger. He then winked at Chingu and added, "Perhaps you're right. Maybe he did die, but that's neither here nor there. What should concern you is whether

Jack Frost remained dead."

Drizzle chimed in, "That's not possible!"

"It isn't? Then tell me the name of the one that pursues you, even now," the tiger added.

"Theran!" Cloud answered. "I knew he was powerful, but not powerful enough to bring someone back from the dead." Shock and disbelief were written all over his face.

"Maybe not, but almost dead isn't the same as dead. That's all I can say on the matter," answered the informant.

"This is bad! This is really bad!" Chingu commented. "We have to find him and finish the job!"

"Great idea! Tell me, how do you plan to do this? Do you even know where he is?" asked the tiger.

"No, but I have a way to find out,"

Chingu replied. He turned to his brother and said, "Shinyuu, come with me." The red pandas walked out the door together.

Cloud focused his attention back on the tiger and resumed their conversation. "Back to the matter at hand. We need a ship."

"If I give you one, what guarantee do you give me that you won't get it shot to bits, or worse? You've already lost your own ship." Then with a grin, the tiger added, "Let's not count your father's ship, or you'll be two for two."

"I can't give you one, but I vow to repay you with two ships, if something were to happen to it," Cloud answered back.

"That won't be necessary!" came a loud voice from the back of the bar. A cloaked figure stood up and removed his hood. It was none other than Cloud's first mate,

Brynjar. He stood tall and was arrayed with armor from shoulder-to-shoulder. He threw his cloak back over his shoulder and approached his captain.

Cloud could not have been happier. They exchanged hefty bear hugs before Brynjar continued. "Captain, I and a few others have been searching for you for so long. It does my heart glad to see you alive! We have a new ship and named her Mjölnir, in memory of our old ship. The vessel's a beauty, and she's waiting for us, just off shore."

As their conversation continued, Flurry observed closely. He was suspicious of Cloud's first mate. It was oddly convenient that he just happened to be there and had a ship. Flurry decided to keep his thoughts to himself, but he was not going to let Brynjar out of his sight.

Cloud looked back at the tiger and addressed him by name. "Talvist, until next time ..." but his sentence was cut off as a cannonball crashed through the front window and out the back wall, followed by a loud *BOOM!*

"We're under attack!" shouted the barkeeper. The pub patrons ran in every which direction. The scene became utter chaos as drunk patrons scrambled for their lives.

BOOM! came another loud and thundering sound of another cannon. Before long, cannon fire became so frequent that it was clear that the small town was about to be wiped from the map.

Flurry and his gang rushed out and saw longboats pulled up on the beach. Grizzly bears exchanged blows with Cloud's polar bear crew. Black Bear'd had found them!

The chaos was extensive. Flurry had no idea where Chingu or Shinyuu were. The polar bear crew was widely dispersed, and he had a tough time keeping tabs on Cloud. Flurry turned to Noah and asked, "Can you keep an eye on everyone for me? There's something I have to do." Before Noah could even respond, Flurry ran off into the battle.

The buildings billowed smoke as flames engulfed the town. Cannons continued to fire from the Arctos. Cast-iron balls impacted all around Flurry while he ran across the battlefield. He had to catch up with Cloud. He could not allow anything to happen to the captain. Flurry was not sure why, but he had a gut feeling about Brynjar that he had to pursue.

Drizzle arrived with the gang. He had his

ears covered and looked like he was going to cry. Drizzle was having a really hard time dealing with so much happening all around him. The bar environment was taxing enough on his senses. He felt like he was living his worst nightmare. He shouted to the others, "We need to find a safe place to hide! Follow me!" Drizzle ran off toward the forest with Noah, Caboose, Boaz, and Honja close behind.

Yelling and screaming could be heard as the town became a pile of burning rubble. The sound of metal-on-metal resounded as sword battles raged on. The inhabitants of the town had joined the fight. They were not inclined to be on Cloud's side, but they were now in a fight for their own lives. Black Bear'd had a fearsome reputation for leaving no survivors.

Flurry watched as Cloud and Brynjar fought back-to-back. It was like the captain and first mate were of the same mind in combat. They made quite a team as they took down one enemy after another.

The cub scanned the crowded beach until he finally spotted Shinyuu and ran toward him.

The red panda continued to fight without the use of his sword. Flurry began to think it was merely decoration and that Shinyuu did not even know how to use a sword. Flurry was a few steps away when someone grabbed him.

"Put me down!" he shouted and repeatedly struck his captor on the arm.

"Flurry, stop! It's just me," answered the assailant. Flurry looked up, and to his relief he saw Chingu. "What are you doing here?"

the red panda asked. "You need to get to safety with the others."

"I don't know where they are," Flurry replied.

"Come on! I'll help you find them," answered Chingu.

"No! I can't! I'm watching out for Cloud."

"He's very capable. He'll be fine."

"That's not what I mean!" replied the cub. Chingu sat Flurry back on his feet and looked at him for an explanation. "I don't know why, but I have a bad feeling about his friend." Flurry pointed at Brynjar.

Chingu was not in the tavern when Brynjar showed up, but it was clear that he was a part of Cloud's crew. "What about him?" Chingu asked.

"The tiger said that Theran can control the

minds of others with his ring. What if it's a trap for Cloud?"

Chingu looked back at Brynjar and considered Flurry's theory as a genuine possibility.

"I'll bet you that we'll all escape on his ship without anyone being killed or captured. Mark my words. It seems all too con-vent."

"You mean convenient?" Chingu asked.

"Yeah, that's what I said!" Flurry replied.

At that moment, Theran and his crew arrived from the forest behind the town. The snow leopard stood by and watched the battle rage on. Chingu took note of how Theran did not try to use any of his powers, but simply observed.

Brynjar and Cloud were met by more polar bears that had arrived from their new ship. They shouted, "This way! We have a way out! Hurry!"

Chingu was convinced. He whistled for his brother. Shinyuu took his enemies to the ground before he rushed to Chingu's side.

"Yes?" asked Shinyuu.

Chingu gave his brother a stern look and said, "I need you to do exactly as I ask. Do you understand?"

"Sure!" Shinyuu replied.

"I'm serious!"

"I know. I promise."

"Take Flurry and go join Drizzle and the others. I believe I saw them sneak off into the forest over there," Chingu instructed.

"What about you?" Shinyuu asked.

"I'm going to sneak aboard the escape ship. Something's not right about this. After the battled subsides, take the others and head to Amur. Get a ship, and sail to Amoy."

"With what? We don't have any mon …" Shinyuu's words were cut short when Chingu put two coins in his paw. The red panda nation of Nallan Min was among the wealthiest kingdoms. Just one of their coins could easily buy an entire ship.

"Okay, now go!" Chingu ordered before he turned and ran out to one of the longboats. He glanced back and shouted one last command. "Please make sure nothing happens to Flurry or the others! You're honor bound to protect them all!"

Shinyuu bowed, grabbed Flurry, and ran toward the tree line as Chingu seized a boat and shoved off. Flurry looked over Shinyuu's shoulder and wondered if that would be the last time he would see Cloud or Chingu ever again.

CHAPTER 6
MUTINY

Waves sloshed to and fro against a beautiful, new ship. It was absolutely pristine, as if it had just been built that very day. The vessel had blue accents in various places and intricate knotwork designs carved into the side of the hull. The same artistic expression decorated the doors, rails, and even the three masts that upheld the beautiful blue and white sails.

The ship was a close match to the Arctos. Both were warships with twenty cannons on each side, divided among two decks. Cloud was well-pleased with the new ship. He knew that if he were to face off against Black Bear'd again, the odds would now be in his favor, or at the very least it would be a fair fight.

The first Mjölnir belonged to Cloud's father, before he and his crew were murdered by Black Bear'd and his ship torched. Cloud had made it his mission to stop Black Bear'd at all costs, but in their last battle the evil grizzly captain bested him and burned Cloud's ship, which he had named Mjölnir in loving memory of his father's vessel.

They say good things come in threes. Maybe the third ship to bear the name would be the one to bring victory to his crew, justice for his father, and vengeance to quench Cloud's thirst for revenge.

Cloud looked out over his new ship as they sailed over the endless blue below. "Where to next, captain?" inquired his first mate. He stood at attention.

Cloud now looked the part of a captain. He had cleaned up and was dressed in leather boots, brown pants, and a blue captain's coat with armor plating on the shoulders. At his side was his sword and his battle horn. On his back he carried a round wooden shield. All of his attire was accented with decorative knotwork.

"Set course for Amoy! We shall gather there and make plans before we go after Black Bear'd," the captain commanded.

"Aye, aye, sir!" replied Brynjar.

Audun stood nearby. After he heard the captain's orders, he felt the need to speak up. "Captain, if I may speak freely?"

"Go ahead," Cloud replied.

"Black Bear'd is important, but are not also our friends? Shouldn't we seek to find what became of the cubs and your friend Shinyuu?"

Cloud smiled and replied, "I have faith in Shinyuu. He fools around too much, but he's very capable, and he'll know to meet us at Amoy."

"Forgive me, captain, but how can they get to Amoy without a ship?"

Cloud shot him a glance that communicated he was losing his patience with the questions.

Audun caught the hint and backed away. "I'm sorry, captain. Forget I asked." As Audun walked away, he felt that something was wrong. He knew his captain well, and he was not behaving like a leader with a sound mind.

Now below deck, Audun spoke quietly with the rest of the crew. One-by-one he pulled them aside to have a talk. "Have you noticed the captain behaving strangely?"

Stian looked at him and typically would have kept silent, but that time he broke his silence. "You know me. I'm not one to speak ill of our captain, but I think his thirst for revenge has gone to his head."

"I agree. We should count our blessings. We were freed from Black Bear'd's grip. We rescued the captain, and survived the attack from last night. We've been reunited with our long-lost shipmates, and everyone survived. We even have a new ship. There's no need to tempt fate by intentionally chasing down trouble," Auden replied.

"Then on top of that …"

"Shhhhh!" Stian cut off his comrade as one of their missing crewmates walked by. They politely nodded to each other. Stian turned back to Audun and whispered, "How many of the crew have you spoken with?"

"I don't know. Maybe five or six, why?"

"Were any of them from the group that rescued us?"

"No. I don't believe so. I had planned to tell them, too, but they haven't been as social as they used to be. Is there a problem?"

"Everything feels strange. I don't trust them. Let's keep this quiet until we know more."

"Agreed." They shook and parted ways.

From the outside of the ship, Chingu listened in and observed everyone. Chingu was disturbed to know that it was not only he and Flurry who had a bad feeling about how the battle had turned out. As the red panda held tightly to the outer hull of the ship, he wondered how Shinyuu and the others were doing.

Numerous hours had passed since the battle. The sun was up in the sky, and Shinyuu safely brought Flurry and the others all the way to Amur. The trip took twice as long due to all of the breaks the cubs needed.

The city was breathtaking. Drizzle had just been to Amur not too long ago, but for Flurry and the others it was so fresh and amazing. They all looked around and gazed at the beautiful oriental architecture. It was clear that Amur was also governed by the same tigers that ruled over Tigris.

Many of these tigers wore elaborate, decorative clothing. The female tigers wore robes of silk in a diverse array of vibrant hues of turquoise, red, white, or violet.

As they traveled the streets of Amur, Flurry and the others were obviously exhausted and dragged their feet with each step. The previous evening was the longest night Flurry could ever remember. Never had he needed to walk or run so much, and his tummy grumbled fiercely.

Shinyuu led them to his favorite inn named "The Fox 'n a Sweater." Shinyuu and Drizzle had spent some time there not long ago. Once inside, the entire group decided to take care of the first order of business. "Food!" Flurry cheerfully exclaimed when a server brought plates of hot, steaming goodness.

The cubs wasted no time before they dug right into their meal. It appeared as if Flurry and Drizzle were in a competition to find out who could eat the most in the least amount of time. Noah pretended to drink from his empty mug. He had no need to eat, but he liked to play along. In fact, none of the plush animals needed food, but they had grown accustomed to it. Flurry particularly loved to savor the variety of different flavors. It was a good thing he was just a teddy bear, or else he would never be able to eat as much as he did. For Flurry, eating was one of the greatest pleasures life had to offer him.

Luckily for Shinyuu, money was no object. With just one coin he could have purchased the entire inn for himself. Prior to their arrival, he met with a merchant and exchanged his single coin for many bags of coins that he dispersed among the others, so they could buy whatever they wanted.

When they had finished their feast, Drizzle had one last muffin that sat on his plate. He stared it down as if it were an enemy to be conquered. He was not sure if he could handle the challenge. His stomach ached, and he felt like he could not take another bite. In fact, he felt like he might be sick if he looked at it any longer.

Flurry reached for the muffin. "If you aren't going to eat it, I will!"

Drizzle snatched it away and stuffed it in his mouth.

"Pig!" Flurry remarked.

Drizzle attempted to mockingly smile at Flurry, but his mouth was stuffed so much that it looked odd.

After their filling meal, they went upstairs

to get a few hours of shut eye before they tried to make their way to Amur's sister city, Amoy.

Typically, Flurry and the others were so full of energy that it took a lot for their mother to get them to calm down and go to bed, but not this day. The cubs could not wait to plop down on the bed, floor, chair, or anywhere else and fall fast asleep.

After a good, long nap, the fuzzies were all awakened by the sound of a knock at their door.

Flurry mumbled, half asleep, "Shinyuu, can you get that?" There was no answer. Flurry sat up, yawned, and rubbed his eyes. He looked around the room, but Shinyuu was nowhere to be found.

Flurry grew concerned. He nudged Drizzle and said, "Drizzle. Drizzle, get up!

Shinyuu's gone!"

"What?" Drizzle exclaimed and shot straight up to scan the room.

Due to the noise, the others awoke and yawned. Flurry rushed to the door, but he could not open it. The doorknob was too high for him. They needed Shinyuu.

"We're going to have to stack some things up to reach it," Drizzle stated.

"Obviously!" Flurry replied.

"Try looking under the bed or in the wardrobe for something we can use."

"Okay, but just so you know, you aren't the boss of me," Flurry informed the other bear cub.

"Would you two just stop it already?" Boaz snapped. "I'm so sick of you two fighting all the time!"

"He started it!" Flurry replied.

"No, I didn't. You did!" came Drizzle's rebuttal.

With a sigh, Boaz got up and joined them. Drizzle looked under the bed, and Boaz checked behind the nightstand. Caboose stared out the window, and Honja sat in the corner with a grumpy expression on his face.

Noah got up and walked over to the door. He was much taller than the rest of them. Flurry followed him to the threshold and stood there as Noah turned the doorknob and pulled the door open. Flurry peeked out through the open crack.

"BOO!" came a loud voice from outside as the door swung open. Shinyuu jumped into the room. Flurry screamed at the top of his lungs and leapt under the bed.

Shinyuu and all of the fuzzies laughed. Flurry was not amused. In fact, he felt both embarrassed and angry. He crawled back out from under the bed. "That wasn't funny! That was really mean, Shinyuu! That was plain mean!" Flurry insisted. His brothers continued to giggle.

Flurry stormed out of the room, and the others gathered their things and followed after him.

Shinyuu and Drizzle went up to the front counter to check out. The owner greeted them. The fox was tall and had vibrant orange fur. Shinyuu handed the fox their room key.

While they waited, Drizzle could not help but ask, "Why is this place named 'The Fox 'n a Sweater' when you aren't wearing a sweater?"

"Everyone's a critic!" exclaimed the irritated fox.

Drizzle was about to speak again when a voice called out to them. "You, there!"

Drizzle looked back and pointed at himself as if he were asking a question. "Yes! You and that red panda!"

Shinyuu turned and saw a familiar face. Without a word, he stepped into a fighting stance, ready for battle.

Laughter broke out from Talvist. The tiger approached Shinyuu and Drizzle with his paws up. "Stand down. I'm not here to cause you any trouble. Fancy meeting you here. I guess my crew weren't the only ones to get the idea to come to Amur."

"What do you want?" Shinyuu replied.

"Want?" Talvist looked at his shipmates and laughed. "Well, the same as you, of course!"

"Which is?"

"Revenge!"

"I'm sorry, but I think you've mistaken us for someone else," came the red panda's reply.

"Come on now, you don't want to get some payback for Black Bear'd capturing your friends?"

"What?" shouted Flurry and Drizzle in one voice.

"Aye! Don't you know? That 'friend' of Cloud's was under Theran's control. I would've warned him right then and there, but as you're aware, we were attacked. After the smoke cleared, they were long gone."

"I'm not saying I believe you, but if I did, we don't even have a ship," Shinyuu replied.

"You have mine. I'll take you," Talvist replied.

"How can we trust you?"

"Ha, ha, ha, ha, ha! I like you! You're funny," Talvist addressed the red panda. "You can't, but what choice do you have? I'm offering you a ship, and you need a ship. Do you have any better deals?"

"We're headed to Amoy. Can you take us there?" Shinyuu asked.

"You bet I can. In fact, I'll do you one better. I'll take you to our pal Cloud so we can save him from his own crew."

"Deal," Shinyuu replied and shook paws with Talvist.

Out at sea, the Mjölnir sailed toward Amoy. The sun stood overhead. Cloud sat in his chair and looked out the back window of his cabin. He had known very few moments of true peace since the day he embarked on his mission to put an end to the evil Black Bear'd. It was nice to have a ship to call his home again.

As he leaned back in his chair, legs propped up on his desk, a knock sounded at the door. "Enter!" the captain shouted.

In came Brynjar with a few other shipmates. "We come bearing gifts for our captain."

Cloud stood up and approached Brynjar, who held a bottle up in front of him. "Care to join us as we celebrate our reunion and the new ship?"

"Indeed! Now that's a valid cause for celebration." Cloud walked out with Brynjar and the others. Egil was at the wheel, and Audun stood near the main mast. "Care to join us?" Cloud asked.

"I'll have to kindly decline, if that's all right by you." Audun answered.

"Very well! More for me then," answered

the captain. He laughed and went below deck.

Audun turned to look at some of the crew he had spoken with. He and Stian nodded to each other before Audun worked his way below deck in pursuit of the captain.

"What's going on?" asked Egil. He looked over at Stian, who stood off to the far left of the brute.

"Nothing," Stian replied.

"I don't buy it. Out with it, or I call the captain," Egil demanded.

Stian filled him in on the plan to protect the captain from Brynjar, but Egil did not buy into it. He reached over, grabbed Stian by the back of his shirt, and dragged him down the steps. Egil was a massive beast of a bear. The rest of the crew feared him. He shouted at another member of the crew and ordered him to take the wheel.

"Let me go!" Stian growled, but it was no use. He could not break Egil's grip.

As he neared the captain and the others, Egil called out, "Captain, it seems we have a traitor onboard." He walked up behind the captain, who was seated at a dinner table with the other crewmembers. When Egil came near, Cloud flopped over, face first onto the table.

"What the …?" Egil stared at his unconscious captain.

Brynjar and three others stood up. "Well now, you weren't exactly supposed to see that." Brynjar aggressively approached Stian and Egil.

"Let me go! We have to stop him!" shouted Stian.

"Agreed!" Egil replied. He loosed his

hold on Stian, out a loud roar, and ran toward Brynjar.

Stian was easily apprehended and knocked out by the other three polar bears. Egil and Brynjar traded blows with each other and wrestled across the table. They made a loud ruckus, but the rest of the crew was above deck. Brynjar called out to any of the other crewmembers for help, but nobody else heard him. The three bears held Egil back and forced him to his knees. "I'm sorry that we've been found out so quickly, but I can't let you inform the others." Brynjar grabbed a beam of wood and struck Egil across the head. He left him unconscious on the floor along with Stian.

Brynjar turned to the others and smiled. "Lock them up with the others! Oh, and be sure to inform Theran that it's done."

CHAPTER 7
CHANGING TIDE

The sun crept toward the horizon. It coated everything in orange. Shinyuu leaned forward and looked out beyond the bow of the ship. He could see the new Mjölnir more clearly as they continued to advance on its position. It seemed to Shinyuu that the Mjölnir either coasted along very slowly, or it was not moving at all. Flurry and the gang sat on the floor of a lower deck and played games.

Flurry felt suspicious again. He did not

know if he should trust his gut or not. *How did Talvist know exactly where to find Cloud?* Flurry questioned in his mind. He turned to the little lion. "Hey, Boaz."

"What is it now, Flurry?" came the lion's annoyed voice. Boaz wrongly assumed that Flurry was going to have something to say that would undoubtedly infuriate him or someone else in the group.

"The ocean's really big, right?"

"Of course, it is! What kind of question is that?"

"How likely are we to just happen to find another ship, if we have no idea where to look?"

"Fairly unlikely, why do you ask?"

"Is it just me, or does anyone else find it odd that Talvist is taking us straight to the ship that Cloud's on? I mean, how does he know where it is? In fact, how did he get to it so fast?"

All of the cubs looked at each other with concerned expressions on their faces. Drizzle glanced over at Flurry. He was impressed with the cub's reasoning. Drizzle then turned toward the group and said, "You know, he has a good point."

"What does this mean for us?" asked Boaz.

Noah pulled out a rope, put it around his neck, and acted as though he were dead. Honja dropped to his side like he had fainted at the idea of more trouble. Boaz then pointed at the rope and said, "See! He's doing it again! Where did Noah get that rope?"

The others looked up, but Noah had already hidden it. "What rope?" asked

Flurry.

"He had a rope! He was acting like he had been hanged! Didn't you see him?"

"Sure he did, Boaz," Flurry answered skeptically.

"I must be losing my mind," replied the lion cub.

"Guys! Focus!" Flurry commanded in a raised voice.

"That's rich, coming from you," Drizzle chimed in.

"Look, I know I haven't exactly been on my best behavior, but this is serious, guys! We're in danger. If they catch us, they might kill us. We have to do something." Flurry's plea struck a chord with the others, and he now had their undivided attention.

"What do you suggest we do?" asked Drizzle.

"Yeah, it's not like we can compete with giant grizzly bears, snow leopards, tigers, panthers, or any other pirates for that matter," Boaz added.

"How do we warn Shinyuu? He's going to be captured, too!" Drizzle spoke with great concern for his friend.

Boaz glanced over to find Noah missing. He panned the room and saw a cardboard box slide across the floor. He could not believe what he was seeing. *How could Noah have gotten a cardboard box?* he speculated.

He decided to let the incident go. He removed his glasses and rubbed his eyes. When he looked back up, Noah was dressed in a ninja outfit and snuck around behind Flurry and Drizzle.

That was it! Boaz could not contain

himself any longer. "Guys, look!"

Everyone turned and found Noah behind them, but without any sign of what he had been up to only moments prior. "What?" Flurry asked.

"He was just dressed up like a ninja and was sneaking around. Before that, he was hiding in a box," Boaz tried desperately to get them to understand that it had really happened, and it was not something he had imagined or made up.

Flurry and Drizzle did not think about it being odd. In fact, it inspired Flurry. "Great idea, Noah! We should hide and then sneak around the ship. We can do some damage that way. We're so small; they'll never be able to find us."

"Hide-and-seek? I love sat game!" Flurry now had Caboose's attention. The polar bear plush was on his feet in no time.

"Wonderful! I'm going to die," Boaz replied with obvious sarcasm at the idea of Flurry or Caboose coming up with plans.

Flurry got up, ran to the open gun port, and peeked his head out. He saw the other ship right beside them. "We're already there! Quick! Everyone follow me!" Flurry shouted.

The cubs all ran after Flurry. They followed the cub behind some crates to hide. Flurry looked around the corner and observed the crew as they conversed. He watched and formulated his plan.

Up above, Shinyuu felt good about how he would get to see Cloud again. As the ship drew near, the red panda's countenance dropped. Behind the Mjölnir, just off of the coastline, sat the Arctos. It had gone unnoticed by the samurai due to it being blocked from sight by an outcropping of some large stones that stood up out of the sea.

"Something wrong?" asked Talvist as he approached Shinyuu from behind.

Shinyuu spun around and reached for his sword. "What's going on here?" he asked.

"I told you I'd take you to meet Cloud. He just happens to be in the custody of Black Bear'd at the moment," came the tiger's sly reply.

Six members of Talvist's crew closed in on the red panda with their swords already drawn. Shinyuu sighed and raised his paws in defeat. Talvist laughed and said, "For a moment there I thought I might actually see you use a sword. What a shame." The rest of his crew laughed. They bound the red panda and prepared to take him over to the Mjölnir.

"Sir! Sir!" shouted a crewmate, who approached Talvist in haste.

"Yes? What is it?" the tiger asked.

"We've searched everywhere. There's no sign of the cubs."

"Search again! They're probably hiding."

"Aye, sir!"

The crew was bound to come up empty-pawed. Flurry and his gang were already on their way over to the Mjölnir. After they had watched Chingu do it with the Arctos many days ago, Flurry and the others took a rope, made a loop at each end, and tossed it over to the Mjölnir's cannon to create a makeshift rope bridge between the two ships.

Flurry went first, followed by Noah, Caboose, Honja, and Boaz. Drizzle brought up the rear. As they boarded the Mjölnir, the rope loosened. When Drizzle had reached the end of the cannon muzzle, the rope came free. Drizzle nearly fell, but clutched onto the cannon lip at the last moment. The cub's paw slipped little-by-little. Drizzle was consumed with fear. He knew that he was about to fall into the ocean.

Flurry climbed back out onto the neck of the cannon, but Noah and the others pulled him back in. "You can't! Someone will see you!" Boaz pleaded.

"I can't just leave him," Flurry replied.

"If we get discovered, we'll be captured, too!"

"All of you go hide! I'll take the risk myself. If we get caught, it will only be the two of us," Flurry demanded. The others obeyed and ran off.

Flurry climbed out onto the swell of the cannon and inched out toward Drizzle. The poor cub gripped the cannon tightly as he hung on for dear life. Flurry crawled on his paws and knees out to the very edge of the cannon and reached out for Drizzle. "Give me your paw," Flurry whispered, so that they would not be discovered by anyone from up above.

"I can't. I can't. I'm slipping. Flurry, help me!" Drizzle called out in deep distress.

Flurry got onto his belly, reached down for Drizzle's paw, and grabbed him, just as he was about to fall. "Gotcha!" Flurry reassured his friend, but Drizzle was heavier than Flurry expected. The cub huffed and puffed as he tried to pull Drizzle up. "Man, you are heavy! You really shouldn't have eaten that last muffin!" Flurry grunted and pulled as hard as he could.

Drizzle's paw inched its way out of Flurry's grip. It was clear that he was about to fall. They both panicked. "Please, don't drop me!" Drizzle pleaded.

Flurry sweat heavily. He realized the inevitable truth; he could not hold on much longer. Suddenly, Drizzle's paw slipped free. "No!" Flurry shouted, but Drizzle did not fall. When Flurry saw Drizzle hover in place, he turned around and found Chingu as he dangled from a rope up above them. The red panda held on to Drizzle's belt and lifted him back up onto the cannon.

The cubs quickly crawled inside, followed by Chingu. "Chingu!" they both exclaimed and gave him a group hug.

"I'm so glad to see you!" Flurry exclaimed.

"That's an understatement," Drizzle added.

Chingu looked out to see if anyone had noticed them, but they seemed to be in the clear. He turned back to the cubs and asked, "How did you escape the other ship?"

"We didn't have to. I suspected something was wrong, so we hid," Flurry replied.

"Good thinking!" Chingu replied.

"Yeah, good job, Flurry!" came an unexpected compliment from Drizzle as he patted Flurry on the back. "And thanks for the save, too."

Flurry looked back at Chingu and continued. "We just barely escaped, though. I think Shinyuu got captured."

Chingu dropped his chin and shook his head before he replied, "Why am I not surprised? If there's one thing he's good at, it's getting captured."

"So what's the plan?" Drizzle asked.

"I'm not sure. What do you think?" replied the red panda.

"I've got nothing," Drizzle answered.

"I think I have an idea," Flurry commented. The cub had a sly look on his face.

Black Bear'd's ship now approached from the port side of the Mjölnir with Talvist's ship on the starboard side. They were trapped. It seemed like impossible odds, but Flurry sent Drizzle and Boaz to rig some of the cannons to go off at a precise time.

Flurry and Chingu rushed to the brig to free Cloud and any other prisoners. Noah kept watch while Caboose and Honja hid and waited for further instructions.

Cloud and his crew sat on the deck floor, chained up. They found themselves back in the same situation they had started in. Cloud felt like a fool. With his head hung low, his humiliation was apparent. The captain thought about Brynjar giving him to Black Bear'd as a trophy. He had trusted his first mate with his very life. He could not believe what had happened.

Cloud's thoughts were interrupted at the sound of the door being unlocked. He half expected Black Bear'd to walk in, but to his delight, it was Chingu and Flurry.

"What are you two doing here?" he asked with both enthusiasm and caution. "How did either of you even get aboard, let alone into the brig?"

"Shhhhh! No time for explanations. Listen closely, Flurry has a plan," Chingu answered the polar bear captain and unlocked his shackles.

Flurry went through parts of his plan while Chingu freed the rest of Cloud's crew. Before Flurry could go into very much detail, the sound of footsteps approached.

"Quickly! Hide!" Chingu whispered. The red panda took cover in a corner with Flurry. The polar bears sat back down and pretended to remain chained up.

The door creaked open, and in walked Shinyuu, closely followed by one of Cloud's mutinous crew. It was clear that the polar bear guard was under Theran's control.

Before the guard had any opportunity to lock up his new prisoner, Cloud rushed up, tackled him, and knocked him out. His crew came to his aid to lock up the guard and then armed themselves.

With their armor and weapons ready, they made their way up deck-by-deck. Along the way, they knocked out any of the Theran-controlled crew and locked them up with the rest of the others. Egil officially stood watch to prevent anyone from getting in or out.

Flurry reconvened with his friends at the base of the steps up to the main deck.

"The fuses are set," Drizzle informed him.

"Good," Flurry replied. "How long do we have?"

"About five minutes, maybe less."

"Okay, here's what we're going to do ..."

Flurry's words were cut short when Cloud interjected. "Oh no! It's him!"

Everyone looked up the steps and saw Theran as he walked around on the main deck. Then another pirate caught Cloud's attention. "Talvist! What's he doing here?"

"Like we said, it's a long story," Chingu replied.

"Let's just say he's one of the bad guys," Flurry chimed in.

"This is never going to work," Cloud replied. "I mean, we're greatly outnumbered on and off of the ship. It's two ships against one, and a majority of my crew is under Theran's influence."

"Not for long," Flurry replied confidently.

"What are you up to?" Boaz asked suspiciously.

Flurry looked at the lion cub, grinned, and replied, "Is there anything sticky on this ship? I'm looking for something that's almost like glue."

"There's pitch," answered Audun.

"What's sat?" asked Caboose.

"It's tar that's used to waterproof the ship and stop leaks," Boaz replied.

"That's perfect!" Flurry exclaimed. "Drizzle, I'll need you to throw tar right at Theran's mouth. Do you think you can hit the target?"

"Of course I can. Why?"

"That'll prevent him from talking. Then, that's when Cloud attacks and keeps him busy. That'll be my cue to rush in and steal his ring. After I break the ring, we'll have more of Cloud's crew to fight on our side."

"This is very risky," Cloud replied. "You're putting yourselves in grave danger. I can't allow little cubs to do something so risky."

"It won't be risky, I'll have Chingu to protect me," Flurry replied.

"No, you won't. Somebody has to keep

your enemies at bay. Besides, what if Black Bear'd's up there, too?"

"Oh, yeah, I didn't think about that."

"Shinyuu will protect you," Chingu suggested.

Surprised, Shinyuu pointed to himself and said, "Me? Why me?"

"Shinyuu, I'm counting on you. Don't mess this up!"

"I won't!" Chingu's brother replied.

Chingu then got up and walked off to get into position.

"What about us?" asked Boaz.

Flurry addressed them and said, "Boaz, your job is to help Drizzle and to make sure our plans with the cannons work. Honja, when I get the ring, I'm going to hand it off to you. Nobody can catch you."

Honja shook his head vigorously in

protest.

"Come on, Honja! You've done it before. Remember the crystal?" Flurry reasoned.

"It's okay. You'll be fine. You can do this," came Boaz's pep talk. Honja spoke with Boaz in his own tongue, and eventually he reluctantly agreed.

"Great!" Flurry answered.

"Uh, Flurry!" Drizzle chimed in. "Those cannons are going to fire at any moment now. I hope you're about to wrap this up."

"Okay, Caboose …"

"Sat's me!" replied the plush polar bear.

"You'll be a distraction."

"Ohhh! What's sat?" Caboose replied.

Flurry smacked himself in the forehead and then amended his order. "Never mind. I know! We're going to play a game," Flurry began.

"Yay! I love games!"

"I want you to follow Honja up to me after I get the ring. Then you and Honja run away in different directions."

"Okay. So what do I do again?"

"Never mind, just run around. Don't let anyone catch you!"

"Yay!"

"And, Noah ..." *BOOM!* sounded the first of many cannons that fired from both sides of the ship. In the heat of the moment Flurry quickly added, "Just wing it!"

Chaos had broken loose. Pirates from both enemy vessels boarded the Mjölnir to avoid going down with their ships. Talvist's ship was sinking, and the Arctos was on fire. Black Bear'd was livid. He grabbed a rope and swung across to the Mjölnir.

"I see it's another one of your screwups!" he shouted at Theran.

"This has nothing to do with me!" the snow leopard snapped back at the grizzly bear.

Black Bear'd made his way toward the steps, but was met by Chingu with his sword drawn.

"Chingu, be careful!" Drizzle called out to his friend.

"Hurry! We have to act fast!" Flurry shouted. "Drizzle! Now!"

Drizzle reached into a bucket of black, sticky tar, attempted to make a ball out of it, and threw it right at Theran's mouth.

Theran was taken aback and dropped his staff. He franticly attempted to wipe the pitch from his mouth. The more he messed with it, the more it stuck to his fur. He barely had a chance to recover before Cloud stormed out from below with a war cry and slammed into the snow leopard.

Theran was very strong. He could have easily fought Cloud and won, but he had been caught off guard, and he had a hard time breathing with the pitch on his snout.

Cloud punched Theran in the face while Chingu held Black Bear'd off. The grizzly pirate captain was far stronger than Chingu. Just one hit, and it would be over for the red panda. However, Black Bear'd was full of rage and lacked the self-control the Protector had spent years mastering. Chingu was extremely nimble. He ducked under Black Bear'd's sword, dodged his punches, and leapt over his lunges.

Flurry saw his chance and ran out into the raging battle as Cloud's crew fought Talvist's. Black Bear'd's crew made their way over to the Mjölnir to join in the fight.

Flurry was about to make it to the base of the steps, but Shinyuu grabbed him by the scarf. "Stop! It isn't safe!" Shinyuu ordered the teddy bear cub and pulled him to cover.

"Obviously! But somebody has to get that ring!" Flurry replied.

"We go together. I'll protect you," Shinyuu replied.

"Shinyuu! This isn't the time for jokes!"

"I'm not joking!"

"Come on! Chingu's the awesome fighter. He told me the thing you're good at is being captured."

"Yeah, I suppose ..." Shinyuu paused midsentence and said, "Wait a minute! He said that?"

"Uh huh!"

"My brother said that?"

"Yep!"

"Are you sure?"

"Yes, he said so."

Shinyuu then remembered the mission, snapped out of his preoccupation with his brother's statement, and refocused. He looked into Flurry's eyes and said, "Just trust me! Stay here and wait for my signal, okay?" Flurry relented and nodded his head in affirmation.

As Shinyuu finished his instructions, eight of Black Bear'd's crew boarded the Mjölnir. The grizzly bears closed in on Cloud's crew.

Shinyuu rushed out onto the deck and shouted, "Hey!" The grizzly bears turned toward him and drew their swords.

The next moments took Flurry by surprise. His jaw fell open when he beheld a sight he never expected to see. Shinyuu pulled his samurai sword from its scabbard and confronted the pirates.

One-by-one, Shinyuu's enemies fell by his blade. He moved so fast that he appeared to be a blur. Left and right, pirate after pirate collapsed. Shinyuu cut his enemies down with ease.

"Wow! He's amazing!" Flurry exclaimed to himself while he watched in awe.

After more than ten pirates were slain by the red panda's blade, he shouted, "Flurry! Now!"

Flurry mustered every ounce of his courage as he, Honja, and Caboose ran out onto the deck of the ship. Flurry took the lead and ran straight for Theran.

Cloud and Theran were still in a fist fight. It was clear that Cloud was the victor. He pummeled the snow leopard repeatedly. Theran could barely catch his breath. Flurry ran up to Theran's dangling arm, grabbed the ring, and sped off. As he ran off, he called back, "Thanks! Okay, goodbye!"

Cloud grabbed Theran by the robe and threw him overboard. "Now, that was satisfying," he added and then focused his attention on Black Bear'd. He pulled out his sword and nodded at Chingu. The red panda did a double backflip to distance himself from the battle. Cloud ran toward the evil grizzly bear and swung his sword at him. White Cloud and Black Bear'd were now locked in a rage-fueled swordfight.

Flurry ran with the ring safely in his paw. Different pirates tried to catch him, but he tossed the ring to Honja, who darted off in an alternate direction. Another pirate pursued the rabbit, but Honja was so little that it was hard to keep track of him amidst the chaos. Before the guard could blink, Honja changed course.

"Here! Throw it here!" shouted Flurry at the rabbit.

Honja tossed the ring back to Flurry, and they both ran down the steps and met up with the others. Flurry did not waste any time. He proceeded to smash the ring with one of the cannonballs. He beat the gemstone that adorned the ring as hard as he could. The stone shattered into hundreds of pieces. A burst of bright, purple light shot out from the broken shards and faded away.

"Drizzle!" Flurry shouted. "Run to the brig and release Cloud's crew!"

"Aye, aye, captain!" Drizzle saluted. The gesture brought a smile to both of their faces.

The fight was off to a good start, but things now looked bleak for Cloud, Chingu, Shinyuu, and the four other polar bears under Cloud's command. They were each valiant warriors, but the few of them could not hold off such numbers.

Talvist's ship had sunk entirely. He unceasingly fought against Chingu, though only a few from his crew still lived. Black Bear'd's crew was numerous, and they continued to come aboard while the Arctos sat ablaze in the water.

Drizzle ran up to Egil and shouted, "Flurry destroyed Theran's ring. Are they back to being their old selves again?"

Egil opened the door and saw the polar bear crew back in their right minds and struggling to free themselves. "Let us out of here! We have to save the ship!" shouted the first mate.

Egil and Drizzle ran over and uncoupled their restraints. The crew had been restored. They grabbed their weapons and joined the battle.

With a loud bay of a battle horn, Brynjar and the remaining crew surfaced and made short work of Black Bear'd's crew.

Boaz, Honja, Drizzle, and Flurry met back up under the ropes around the main mast. "Okay, is everyone here?" Flurry asked.

"No, Caboose and Noah are still out there somewhere," answered Boaz.

Flurry bent down and patted Honja on the head. "Good job, my friend," the bear informed his rabbit brother. Honja quickly pushed Flurry's paw away. Flurry grinned uneasily before he looked up and saw Caboose.

"Ahhhhh!" shouted the polar bear plush as he ran past. A pirate chased Caboose all over the ship, back and forth across the deck. Noah had grabbed a broom handle and used it as a staff. Noah tripped or struck various enemies in order to rescue Caboose and bring him to safety.

The battle raged on as Cloud and Black Bear'd exchanged blows. Their swords clashed, and Cloud continued to advance. He pushed Black Bear'd out onto the plank. Their swords swept back and forth as they each fought for their lives.

Cloud knocked the sword from Black Bear'd's paw and stood there with the tip of his blade pointed at the grizzly bear's nose.

"It would seem that you've lost," came

Captain White Cloud's remark.

"No, I haven't! It isn't over until it's over!" Black Bear'd responded vehemently.

"Well, a ship for a ship. You burned mine, now I've burned yours. Until next time."

"Indeed," said the grizzly and stepped off of the plank. The evil pirate plunged into the cold waves down below.

"Did you just see what he did?" Shinyuu asked.

"I guess it's better than dying by the sword," Chingu replied.

"Coward!" Cloud added. "This means that we'll be seeing him again."

"Maybe. If a shark doesn't eat him," Shinyuu interjected.

Everyone turned and looked at him with a blank expression on their faces. Shinyuu looked up and was surprised that everyone had their eyes fixed on him. "What? We can always hope, right?"

Flurry intervened. He ran up and said, "What's important is that we won!"

The crew shouted and blew their battle horns. "Hooray!" came their celebratory shouts.

Everyone had been defeated, and the only enemy left on the ship was Talvist. The tiger was on his knees before Chingu's sword.

"What shall I do with you?" Cloud asked as he approached. "Strange. I thought we were friends, but I guess you sold us all out, didn't you?"

"Cloud, please understand. It wasn't personal. If I didn't, Black Bear'd would've killed me," answered the tiger.

"What do you think I'm about to do?"

Cloud raised his sword.

Talvist closed his eye and held up his paws in front of his face. "No! No! Please don't! Oh, please! Have mercy!" He screamed and cowered on his knees.

The death-delivering blow never came. Talvist peeked and saw Cloud still standing there.

"Luckily for you, I'm merciful. That's what separates me from the likes of you and Black Bear'd," Cloud answered.

The captain put his sword away and walked a few steps off. He paused, and turned back. "However, that doesn't mean I have to keep you on my ship." Cloud kicked Talvist in the chest. The tiger fell over the side and into the cold water.

"If you ask nicely, maybe Black Bear'd will share part of his ship for you to float on!" Shinyuu shouted and giggled to himself.

The crew cheered. They had victory at last! With the crew united, they set sail.

Nighttime came. The moon and stars lit up the sky. A cool breeze blew across the deck as the ship sailed to Tigris. Down below, much merriment took place.

The crew shouted, laughed, cheered, and exchanged embellished stories of their fight. Flurry and his friends sat at a smaller table, ate delicious food, and shared funny stories with each other.

"You know, you did a great job as leader today," Drizzle informed Flurry.

"Thanks! Your plans were pretty good, too," Flurry replied. "Oh, by the way, what was that really loud noise the night you and Boaz set your trap on that ship?"

"We improvised. You know the fuses that set off the cannons?"

"Uh huh."

"Well, I led another fuse straight to all of the gunpowder. I thought it would be best to prevent them from getting another ship."

"You really are a genius," Flurry replied. "I'm glad that none of your plans involved falling over a wall this time."

"Hey!" Drizzle shouted. They both looked at each other and giggled.

Off in another corner, Chingu approached his brother. "I have to congratulate you."

"For what?" asked Shinyuu.

"You went above and beyond the call of duty. I'm proud of you for protecting Flurry and the others the way you did. I know you don't like to fight, but you did the right thing today." Chingu reached over and patted

Shinyuu on the shoulder.

"Thanks," Shinyuu replied with a smile.

Chingu stood up and turned to walk away. Shinyuu asked, "Where are you going?"

"To get a drink. Do you want anything?"

"How about this?" Shinyuu asked. Chingu turned and saw a pie fly through the air straight at his face. Chingu quickly ducked, and the pie hit Captain White Cloud. Sudden silence came over the entire room.

Cloud wiped the pie away from his eyes, looked over at the guilty party, and shouted, "Shinyuu!"

Laughter broke out as Cloud chased Shinyuu around the room. That night was one of the best nights Flurry had ever experienced. There was so much joy, laughter, and camaraderie. He felt like he was truly with friends. In fact, he viewed them as family.

After about a week at sea, they arrived in Tigris. Flurry and his friends bade farewell to Captain White Cloud and his crew.

Most of the gang were quick to step foot on solid ground again, but Drizzle noticed Flurry's absence. He turned back to investigate and found Flurry below deck. Drizzle stood and watched as Flurry emptied out the contents of his bag. Drizzle cleared his throat, which startled Flurry.

"What are you doing?" Drizzle asked.

"Oh, nothing," Flurry replied. "How long have you been standing there?"

"Long enough."

"I feel bad for stealing all of this stuff, so I'm leaving it here. Being a pirate isn't as great as I hoped it would be. I don't want to be a bad bear, or carry around stolen stuff," answered Flurry. He grabbed the golden statue from the pile of his discarded treasure and put it back into his bag.

"Wait a minute! I thought you said you were putting it all back," Drizzle chimed in.

"What? This? Oh! I've made up my mind to find out where it belongs and return it to them. Something this cute is surely missed by its owner," Flurry answered.

Drizzle smiled and walked up the steps. Flurry ran over to join him. He tugged on Drizzle's belt and asked, "Where did you get this?" The strap that held Drizzle's sword was different than before. It was now elaborately decorated with red knotwork down its length.

"This?" Drizzle replied. "Oh, it's a gift from Captain White Cloud. He said it's a thank you for all I did for him and his crew."

Normally, such an answer would have made Flurry jealous, but he looked down at his golden statue, back up at Drizzle, and smiled as they disembarked together.

Chingu followed close behind. He paused, turned back to Cloud, and asked, "How about you? What will you do now?"

"I'm going to follow up on some leads," answered the captain. "Brynjar tells me that Theran and Black Bear'd have been recruiting able-bodied warriors to build an army. I mean to find out where they are and who this army is for."

"An army?" Chingu asked.

"Yes. It turns out that we still don't know who Theran and Black Bear'd were working for."

"Talvist said it was Jack Frost."

"Talvist is a liar. I'll believe it when I see it for myself," answered the captain.

"If you find it to be true, inform me right away. We can't have a threat like that go unchallenged."

"I will indeed. You have my word."

Chingu left the ship, and they all waved goodbye as White Cloud and his crew sailed off.

The morning was very beautiful with the autumn trees vibrantly adorned. The first thing Flurry wanted to do was eat. Shinyuu and Chingu took the cubs to the market to get food and then walked to a set of stables to pick up their transportation.

"I hope she's all right. We left her here so long ago," Drizzle whispered to Shinyuu as Chingu opened a stall door.

A large reeyu stepped forward. It had

large wings, spikes that lined its tail, and three sharp horns on top of its head. At the sight of Flurry, it charged toward him.

Flurry turned and ran in fear. The reeyu caught him, knocked him to the ground, and licked his face.

The bear screamed. "Help! Help! It's going to eat me! It's eating me now! I can feel it!"

The gang laughed heartily. Drizzle rushed over and pulled the reeyu away. With a giggle, Drizzle said, "Faith's just happy to see you again."

"Faith? You mean, that's my reeyu?" Flurry exclaimed with surprise.

"Uh huh," answered Drizzle.

"But, she's so big!"

"Reeyu grow pretty fast," Chingu added.

Flurry felt relieved. He walked back up

and hugged her. She licked Flurry's face as he pet her. Flurry looked up at his reeyu and said, "I missed you, too, girl. I missed you, too."

"All right, everyone up!" came Chingu's command. He and his brother helped Drizzle, Flurry, and the others onto Faith's back.

"Where to now?" asked Drizzle.

"It's time we get everyone home," Chingu replied.

Flurry and his brothers were delighted at the sound of those words. They missed their mother dearly, and they had been gone for far too long. They knew the trip back to Ursus would take a while, but they were finally going home.

EPILOGUE
DARKNESS STIRS

Back in Middleasia, the morning of Flurry's disappearance, Flurry's mother awoke to beautiful rays of the sun that beamed into her bedroom. The light made the purple walls look so calm and relaxing. Lynn wanted to stay in bed. However, she knew she had to deal with Flurry's bad attitude from the night before.

After a brief stretch, followed with a yawn, she sat up and stepped out of her bed. It was clear that her husband had already gone to work, so she went out to the kitchen and boiled a kettle of water. The lady of the house liked to start her morning with a cup of tea.

Lynn poured herself a cup, and while the tea steeped at the table, she decided to check in on her boys. She opened the door and gasped. The room was empty. All five of her boys and their beds were missing.

"Oh no! Oh no! Oh no!" she chanted under her breath. "Where could they be?"

"Flurry! Noah! Boys! Where are you?" she shouted, but there was no reply. She was uncertain what to do. Such a thing had never happened before. She combed the room and searched every nook and cranny of the house, but no trace of her plush children could be found.

She continued speaking to herself out

loud. "Okay, okay, think! There has to be a clue around here somewhere. What can I do?" She dug through Flurry's things and checked his dresser drawers. It seemed hopeless, until she found a small piece of paper with a set of numbers and the word "Santa" on it.

"Hmmm, that's strange. It doesn't look like a phone number," she said to herself. "Worth a try, I guess."

She dialed in the strange group of digits on her phone. A man answered. "Hello?"

"Uh, hi. I hope I didn't dial the wrong number. I know this might sound like a silly question, but is this Santa?"

CLICK Her reply was the sound of the phone being hung up. "Now, that was strange," she said to herself. "So much for that idea."

The young lady sighed and rubbed her face. She had no idea what to do. As she thought about her missing boys, she buried her face in her hands and wept.

She had not been crying for more than a moment when there was a loud knock at the door. "Flurry!" she exclaimed excitedly. Lynn jumped to her feet and ran for the door.

Lynn quickly wiped away her tears and smiled as she anticipated finding her boys at her doorstep. She yanked open the door and her smile vanished. A very tall man with a graying beard and brown eyes stood before her.

He cleared his throat and addressed Flurry's mother. "Mrs. Lee, I presume?"

"Yes?"

"Allow me to introduce myself. My name

is Christopher Kringle."

Shocked, she then asked, "How did you know it was me that called?"

"Flurry is the only one who actually calls me Santa," he replied with a light chuckle.

The oriental beauty gasped and put her hand over her mouth. "Oh, my! Oh, my! Is Flurry with you? Are he and the others okay? Have you seen them?" She could not contain her deeply grief stricken questions.

"No," he began, but paused. He saw clear signs of distress on the young lady's face. After his brief hesitation he added, "Wait a minute. You mean they're all missing?"

"Well, yes. I thought you knew that. Why else would you have come?"

"May I see their room?"

"Of course. Of course. Right this way." The young lady led her guest straight to

Flurry's room.

Christopher looked around before he said, "That's odd. Where do they sleep?"

"This *is* where they sleep, but their beds vanished along with them."

"Really?" Christopher seemed surprised. He looked everything over as he held his chin and analyzed the situation. Then something caught his eye. He quickly rushed over to a box of Flurry's belongings that the cub had kept hidden under his bed.

Christopher reached into the box and lifted out a book with a locked clasp and a crystal embedded into the cover. "*The Book of Snow*," he said. Then he laid the text down and grabbed a small door handle from the box. "The Ayever Del!"

"Excuse me? The what?"

"This is how Flurry can swiftly and easily

travel between our worlds. I gave it to him as a gift back when he first came to visit. I have one just like it."

"I always wondered how he could do that. He never made his travel details very clear to me. So what does this mean?"

"Well, if he doesn't have it with him, it could possibly mean that he's unable to return from wherever he may be."

Tears trickled down the lady's face. "Are the boys okay?"

"I'm willing to bet my life on it. There are things about Flurry that very few know." He turned to the weeping mother and held out his hand. "Come. We have much to discuss. I promise you, we'll find them. I know of just the one to send in search for them."

Flurry's mother stood up and took Christopher's hand. He pulled out a larger, but very similar, door handle from his coat pocket. He placed it against the wall and turned it. Instantly, a door opened up through the wall and led into a dining room she had never seen before. "Welcome to my home," he said. "Don't worry; we'll be back in time to bring your husband up to speed."

The lady of the house rushed over to the closet, grabbed her coat, and rejoined the tall gentleman who patiently waited for her at the mystery door.

Christopher motioned for her to step through first. They both walked through the opening and into a different house. Christopher removed the handle, and the door shut behind them.

*****

Elsewhere, sometime after Black Bear'd's defeat, Theran stood on a small island of solid stone. Not a single plant or animal could be found. On each side of the island, water raged. The river flowed past and over a waterfall that dropped down so far that everything below appeared to be miniature. Theran was at the threshold of a secret entrance to a rumored underground city, named Anesidora.

With some ancient words, Theran spoke, and the stone wall revealed an opening.

The sorcerer made his way down into the deep, dark recesses of a massive cave.

The cave opened up to reveal the cold reality of ice and snow that covered every surface. Some light shone through thick ice in the ceiling, which cast a light-blue hue on everything. The light revealed a massive, underground city. The legends were apparently true.

Theran entered the city through a towering stone archway. Upon his entrance, he observed that the city was full of arctic foxes, snow owls, white wolves, ermines, penguins, seals, and polar bears. Their numbers were beyond his ability to count. It was clear that there was a massive army, and that it had grown in secret.

A palace sat atop of a hill overlooking the rest of the city. He approached the palace door, where he stopped and knocked. The door opened, and Theran entered.

"What news do you have for me?" came a voice that echoed through the room. The interior was very large, with tall walls and a vaulted ceiling.

Theran approached the center of the

room. He looked up at the throne and knelt down before it. "Black Bear'd's ship was destroyed, and my ring was shattered beyond repair," answered the snow leopard.

"And how did this happen, might I ask?"

"We were outnumbered. Captain White Cloud enlisted the help of Chingu the Protector and one of his brothers."

"Really?"

"Yes, master."

"Is that all?"

"No. There were also a number of cubs. They seemed insignificant at the time, but we underestimated them. I think one of them was named Flurry."

"What?" shouted the enthroned figure. He smashed his fists into the arms of his chair. The figure stood up and hastily marched toward Theran.

Theran trembled as the red panda approached. He wore a long, black jacket and had a sword at his side. Theran glanced up at the face of white fur with three scars down his right eye. It was none other than Jack Frost, alive and well.

"That bear has interfered in my affairs for the last time! Go! Find him and destroy him!"

ABOUT J.S. SKYE

J.S. Skye grew up in the Midwestern region of the United States. At a very young age, it was apparent that he was very talented. Finding that he was gifted in music and art, he plunged himself into both. As time passed, he set aside music to focus even more of his attention on developing his skills as an illustrator.

All throughout his years in school, J.S. Skye spent every available moment creating and developing fictional worlds. Caring about realism, he developed multiple people groups, countries, worlds, and even languages. His fictional realms were created through both written and visual mediums.

After traveling to almost a dozen different countries and studying different cultures, J.S. Skye decided to implement his interests in ancient cultures, history, languages, mythology, and more into his writings. He decided it was best to pour his heart and passion into writing instead of having divided interests between both art and literature.

J.S. Skye has accumulated a fairly large collection of his various writings. These stories range from all types of different genres such as mystery, science fiction, fantasy, and even horror. Friends encouraged the aspiring writer to produce a novel and see how things progressed from there.

J.S. Skye's first novel, *The Granted Wish*, was met with cheerful affirmation. The positive feedback was overwhelming and unexpected. Fans of his *Flurry the Bear* novels grew and began to clamor for more. From this point forward, his first novel series came to be.

For more information or to get in touch with J.S. Skye personally, he may be contacted by e-mail at:

JS-Skye@FlurryTheBear.com

ALSO BY J.S. SKYE

Flurry the Bear – The Granted Wish

Flurry the Bear – The Land of the Sourpie

Flurry the Bear – The Throne of Frost

Flurry the Bear – The Book of Snow